Mahagauri

Nitya Neelakantan is a Learning and Development professional, author, and yoga teacher from Bangalore. Her debut novel *Rudrabaan* was self-published in 2021 and is available on Kindle.

Her latest novel *Navapashanam*, published by Readomania in 2023, was one of three finalists at the first-ever Archer Amish Awards for Storytellers. This award was presided over and judged by Lord Jeffrey Archer and Amish Tripathi.

Nitya graduated with a degree in Hotel Management before moving into the learning space. But having indulged in writing poems since a young age, she felt compelled to tell grander stories on larger platforms. And so began her days of writing novels.

When not working, reading, or teaching yoga, Nitya enjoys travelling with her husband, son and furry dog-babies. These travels have helped her gain deep insights into India's folklore, legends, architectural splendours and hidden marvels. India's rich cultural tapestry weaves its way into her stories, where contemporary themes blend seamlessly with mythical elements.

Connect with her:
Instagram: @nityawrites30
X (earlier Twitter): @nityawrites30
Facebook: facebook.com/share/1AwJotJtUk

'*Mahagauri* is a mesmerizing blend of mytho-fantasy and thriller—charting the journey of an ordinary woman caught in an extraordinary collision with destiny. With immersive worldbuilding, a fierce protagonist, and storytelling that feels timeless yet urgent, Nitya Neelakantan's saga grips you from the very first page and refuses to let go. A truly spellbinding work for our times.'

—**K. Hari Kumar**, Author & Screenwriter

Mahagauri

Nitya Neelakantan

RUPA

Published by
Rupa Publications India Pvt. Ltd 2025
161-B/4, Gulmohar House,
Yusuf Sarai Community Centre,
New Delhi 110049

Sales centres:
Bengaluru Chennai
Hyderabad Kolkata Mumbai

This is a work of fiction. Names, characters, places and incidents are either the product of the author's imagination or are used fictitiously and any resemblance to any actual person, living or dead, events or locales is entirely coincidental.

P-ISBN: 978-93-7003-217-0
E-ISBN: 978-93-7003-629-1

First impression 2025

10 9 8 7 6 5 4 3 2 1

Contents

1. A dream blows up in her face 1
2. An ancient kingdom—Saptapuri 10
3. A sacred jewel 13
4. A threat to Saptapuri 19
5. An unforgettable swayamvara 26
6. To the battlefield 32
7. The stranger in the battlefield 39
8. Landing in a nightmare! 44
9. Gauri and the royals 51
10. Shankar—a boy from nowhere 56
11. Universal consciousness and inner-work 62
12. The cruel king from a strange land 77
13. Walking through a ghost town 81
14. The hidden caves 85
15. A general like none other 89
16. The trapdoor in the forest 92
17. The Adiparashakti fortress 98
18. A mighty general 101

19. Reunion at Adiparashakti 106
20. Renewed battle plans 112
21. The training 117
22. Slaying a demon 122
23. A search for Raakat 133
24. The weight of choices 140
25. Betrayal 146
26. A goddess awakens 154
27. A reckoning 168
28. Chaos all around 172
29. Ending darkness 181
30. The sweet smell of victory 197
31. My home, my realm 209

Acknowledgements 213

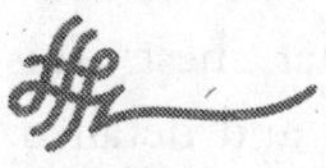

A dream blows up in her face

She crouched behind a boulder, checking that she had all her weapons in place. A sword in its hilt, a dagger tucked into the left side of her waist belt and a poisoned dart pipe at her right. She barely dared to breathe, fearing that someone might detect her.

The forest's thick, close-set trees left almost no room to navigate the ground. The roots had formed clumps the size of small boulders at the base of the trees. High above, the treetops merged into one another, creating a dark canopy that almost blocked out the sun. The sun's rays scattered through tiny gaps that they managed to find between the thick overgrowth. Sunlight danced in tiny circles on the forest floor. She avoided the bright patches to stay hidden. She leaned forward enough over the boulder to check for movement. All was quiet. Just when she thought there was no one around, she heard a faint breath behind her.

She leapt into the air, swung around swiftly, pulled out the dagger from the left side of her waist belt and, even before her feet hit the ground, she slashed the man's throat in one neat line. He dropped to his knees as the sand drank in the blood, turning the place red.

With a start, Gauri sat up in her bed and put her hand to

her mouth to stifle a scream. Sweat drenched her, and her heart thumped wildly as if it wanted to leap out of her chest. This was the first time the dream had been this vivid and detailed. She was still shivering from what she had dreamt about. Though she had just killed someone, yet she had remained so calm.

It was a recurring dream that had haunted her since childhood. It always began in a dark, unfamiliar forest. She seemed to be hiding from someone as she moved stealthily in the shadows. She was always dressed in a saree draped warrior style. The saree below her waist was tucked between her legs to create a pant-style fit. Part of it went over her right shoulder, then was twisted and tucked into the waistband at the back. This freed her hands for quick movement. The strapless blouse was wrapped around her and fastened with a double knot at the back. But what bothered her was the sinister turn the dream had taken today.

Why did this bizarre dream haunt her so often?

As a child, a scared Gauri had run to her mother and shared her dream, and amma had said, 'You are a warrior, *kutti* (little girl). With Appa away so much, you are protecting me just as the Goddess Chamundi protects us all every day.' Gauri had seemed pleased with the theory and tottered off to play.

It was seventeen years since that day. Now she was a grown, working woman living alone in Bengaluru and had no one to calm her after one of her violent dreams. As a senior scientist at a top Indian defence lab, she wanted to know the reason behind it—a logical explanation for this recurring dream that had just turned into a nightmare

Dr Gauri Vishwanath moved through the world like a whisper in a library—quiet, deliberate, and full of hidden stories. Her fingers always carried the faint scent of old paper, ink smudges trailing along the edges of her notebooks like footprints in snow. While others filled their days with chatter, she lingered in the margins, her gaze often lost in the folds of ancient epics and forgotten lore. The Mahabharata wasn't just a tale to her—it was a living, breathing cosmos she wandered through, barefoot and wide-eyed.

At the local orphanage, she was known not for grand gestures but for the way she knelt beside children, her voice a balm, her presence steady as a lighthouse in storm. She once spent an entire night helping a migrant worker find shelter, her own dinner untouched, her phone battery long dead. No one asked her to. No one needed to.

Cinema was her second language. She watched Malayalam thrillers, Marathi dramas, and Assamese romances with the same reverence she gave to Sanskrit verses. Subtitles were optional—she read the curve of a brow, the tremble in a voice, the silence between two glances. Korean and French films played on her screen late into the night, and she'd sit cross-legged, absorbing every nuance like a student of human nature.

Her friends joked that she could tell what someone was feeling before they even spoke. And they weren't wrong. Gauri had a way of tilting her head, narrowing her eyes just slightly, and seeing straight through the scaffolding people built around themselves. She didn't pry. She simply understood.

Gauri got off the bed and made her way in the dark to the kitchen. She turned on the light and fetched herself a glass of water. She sat down at the breakfast counter. It was 2:15 a.m. She thought about the long, arduous day that lay ahead of her. With practically no sleep and a series of experiments she had to wrap up, she already felt it was going to go badly.

Gauri went back to bed. After tossing and turning the entire night, she finally gave up and went for a shower.

After a cold shower, she seated herself in her meditation room and performed her daily yoga. Gauri ended every practice with meditation and the chanting of the sacred *Aum* or *Om*—the primordial sound from which all sounds originated. A combination of three sounds—A, U and M—the word emanates from the belly, moves up through the throat and does not require the use of the tongue.

As a scientist, Gauri had studied and believed that all existence was energy vibrating at various levels. She had read the same explanation in spiritual books as well. She smiled at the thought of science and spirituality aligning in the same direction. As was often the case, her thoughts drifted back to her childhood and her grandparents' home in Thanjavur, the land of the majestic Brihadeeswarar temple.

Gauri had grown up in a traditional Tamil home. Each day, she awoke to the smell of jasmine and incense, and the sounds of the hymn *Bhaja Govindam* or the chanting of *Lalitha Sahasranamam* greeted her. In the 70s, Thanjavur still had a village-like quality to it. Her grandparents' house was a huge, two-storey structure and didn't have boundary walls. A colossal courtyard sat in front and a wooden picket fence, topped with barbed wire, enclosed it. The front door was a huge, hand-carved one. It depicted scenes from Shiva-Parvati *panigrahana*, a Hindu wedding ritual where the groom accepts the bride by taking her right hand in his. These were a replica of the iconic carvings found at the Ellora caves.

Beyond the main door was the central courtyard, typical of houses from the olden days. Verandas ran on all four sides of the courtyard. The house had well-lit, airy and spacious rooms. The walls were adorned with Tanjore paintings of deities, embellished with golden filigree. The courtyard had two large wooden pillars at its centre. A beautiful wooden swing hung from them.

Gauri remembered looking up at her grandpa with wide-eyed awe when he sat on that very swing and narrated riveting stories. They were about various *asuras* or demons and the gods who had vanquished them. She also fondly remembered running around the mango trees in the backyard with her friend Bhadrachalam, enacting those tales.

Every festival was a treat. There was sweet *payasam* and hot *vadai* to snack on and pretty, colourful *pavadai*s to wear. The house was decorated with lamps and lights, and intricately patterned *kolam*s were drawn on the floors outside the doors.

The clock chimed, rudely bringing her back to the present.

Gauri got dressed and rushed to the bus-stand where she waited for her 8:00 a.m. bus to work. As she boarded the bus, her eyes fell on a poster for a new tele serial, *Parashakti*. The poster was a vividly coloured print of a goddess with eight arms atop a majestic lion. Each of her eight arms held a different weapon. The trishul or the trident was the most menacing. It was aimed at a man with a buffalo's head and large, nasty horns. Gauri habitually brought her hands together near her eyes in reverence to Goddess Durga as the bus moved away.

~

'How are you always here before me, babe?' asked Ananya laughingly as she entered the lab and joined Gauri at her workstation.

Gauri and Ananya Deepak had been friends for over five years now. They had both met while interviewing for a junior research fellow position at the Defence Bio-Engineering Labs in Bangalore. They hit it off while waiting to be called in. They became thick friends during their training. Ananya lived in Bangalore with her parents and brother. They lived across the street from the place Gauri eventually moved into after leaving her paying guest accommodation. Both girls had their noses deep in their books for as long as they could remember. This is probably why they had no friends except each other.

'Try the alarm, dear. I hear it works well,' quipped Gauri.

'Yeah, right!' retorted Ananya. Her face with tanned skin and oval jawline twisted into a smirk that portrayed wit.

They both became immersed in their respective work for the rest of the morning. Gauri only looked up when Ananya reminded her that it was time for lunch.

'Listen, I had that dream again, Ani,' said Gauri, tense and cautious, as they sat down for lunch in the cafeteria. Gauri had never shared the details of this recurring nightmare with anyone other than Ananya.

'Are you kidding me, girl? Not THE dream again…' she trailed off. 'What's the big deal about it anyway?'

'Ahem!' Gauri cleared her throat. 'The big deal is that… Don't think I am mad Ani… I killed a man in it this time.'

'Details, please!' asked Ananya, rolling her eyes.

Gauri filled her in on last night's dream and how it had ended this time. Ananya clasped Gauri's hands and said in a soft tone, 'Its ok girl. It was just a dream. You are far too busy with the lab to even go to the movies occasionally, let alone duel someone in a forest. Don't dwell on it.'

'Fine,' said Gauri, in a defeated tone, putting an end to the conversation.

Gauri turned back to her work. She was trying to isolate and purify rare elements such as neodymium from shredded electronic waste using selective precipitation and solvent extraction. This would be useful in manufacturing of high-performance alloys for missile guidance systems.

It was a Friday, so the duo wrapped up work as soon as they possibly could and headed over home to relax.

Gauri brought two cups of tea, and they sat down on the balcony chairs. Gauri's thoughts went back to her dream. She had been feeling very unsettled since the morning.

'Girl, where are you lost? Are you in your fantasy world again? I didn't wrap up work early to watch you moping about how you killed someone in your fantasy. Keep doing that and I'll have to kill you in reality,' said Ananya in all seriousness and with a straight face. And then she smiled and said, 'Lighten up, everything is fine. Now, what are our plans for the evening?'

'Let's watch a movie,' suggested Gauri.

'No.' Ananya replied flatly. 'I am not in the mood for your Tollywood fangirling right now.'

'Okay! I won't make you watch *Baahubali*. We can do a LOTR marathon. You love *Lord of The Rings*, and it has been a while since we watched it last,' said Gauri pleadingly.

She then launched into a tirade over how Ananya had missed the *Hobbit* series in the theatre, and how she had to watch it all alone. Ananya had to put up with five full minutes of Gauri describing Smaug the dragon in excruciating detail.

'If Smaug were real, you would have dated him, right?' Ananya said, laughingly. 'I'm only agreeing because I don't want you to get all mopey about your dream. Let me pop over to my place and get some wine. I have a honey melon-flavoured one that dad gifted me on my birthday. You make the popcorn.'

The two girls settled on the couch with their wine glasses. A huge bowl of popcorn sat in front of them. They clinked their glasses in a toast, and Ananya started the movie. Just as the credits began to roll, Gauri's phone rang.

'Madam, it is me. Charan, from the Lab.'

'What is it, Charan?'

'Ma'am, please come at once. A beaker of liquid from your experiment is hissing and emitting crimson fumes. I don't know what to do.'

Gauri frowned. 'That's strange. The chemical was completely stable when I left this evening. Anyway, I'll be there in twenty minutes,' she told Charan.

'What! You have to go now?' Ananya sounded irritated as her Friday evening plans seemed to go up in smoke.

'I must go to the lab. Something about the liquid I had condensed today. You start without me, and I will be back soon.'

Ananya nodded. Gauri rushed to the lab in a cab. The large clock on the reception wall reminded her of the big ones found on railway platforms. It was 6:25 in the evening. She entered the lab, which was quiet and empty. Charan had gone for a cigarette break after filling her in on the details.

She heard a low hissing noise and saw the beaker on her desk rattling and bubbling up with fumes.

Gauri frowned deeply as she put on gloves to pick up the beaker. It began to emit puffs of crimson coloured smoke. As soon as one faded, a fresh puff arose, like that from a toy train's engine. She was puzzled by the unexpected chemical reaction in the liquid that had remained stable all afternoon.

As she held the beaker, unsure of what to do, a tiny trident from her charm bracelet snapped and fell into the beaker. There was a sudden explosion as the golden trident touched the crimson surface of the chemical. Gauri was engulfed in thick smoke, and her eyes started burning and tearing up rapidly. She began coughing heavily as the beaker slipped through her fingers. She heard the glass shatter, and everything started to spin around her. Her feet jerked as if someone had yanked the ground out from under her. She felt as though she was in free fall, travelling fast through a blur of heavy smoke. She began to scream as loudly as she could, but her voice never left her. It was as if she were frantically screaming inside her own head. Just as suddenly as the explosion had occurred, the smoke cleared out, and she landed with a resounding thud.

An ancient kingdom—Saptapuri

Maharaja Pashupati stood in the *rannaneeti kaksha*, or war room, located at the far end of the south wing of the palace. The room overlooked the flower gardens below. The palace was a masterpiece of architectural splendour. Its interiors had intricately carved wooden pillars and murals of gods and goddesses. The floors were made of polished stone, and the window frames were crafted from multi-coloured mica and sandstone. The royal *shayana kaksha*s, or sleeping chambers, were in the south-west wing of the palace. The queen's bath was situated in the west wing, close to the royal sleeping chambers. It was a covered space with several pipes installed to supply and drain water during the queen's ritual cleansing.

The *mukhya mantrashala*, or royal court, was located in a large central building that also housed the kitchens, dining halls, accommodation for the palace workers and smaller sleeping quarters. The commoner's hall, known as the *praja griha kaksha*, was in a separate complex at the front of the palace. Additionally, there was a beautiful *natyashala*, or hall for performances, which was adorned with mirror work and silver filigree. The hall was designed for the entertainment of the royals, and the king and his courtiers would often enjoy song and dance performances here.

The complex also had an ornately built temple dedicated to different gods. It housed the statues of Vinayaka, the elephant-headed god, Ma Shakti and Lord Shiva.

The palace was surrounded by beautifully manicured gardens featuring water fountains, trees and stone benches. Exquisite flowering shrubs lined the paths, and the gardens bloomed with flowers of almost every hue—pink and white creepers, purple and blood-red rosebuds, delicate orange hibiscus, and indigo pansies and irises. However, the queen's favourite flowers were the yellow bells, which brightened the gardens.

To the far north of the palace was a training ground for men from the court to practice their fighting skills. Adjacent to the training ground, was an important building, the Kabalishwar Vilas.

The palace was magnificent in every way and indicative of a rich culture and a thriving economy. The people of the kingdom of Saptapuri were leading a happy and prosperous life.

And yet, Maharaja Pashupati looked tired and worn out. Age had caught up with him and shrivelled his once muscular body. His face was marked with fine lines and wrinkles surrounded his eyes. He looked up at the portraits of the previous rulers of Saptapuri that adorned the wall. Nine illustrious kings had peacefully ruled Saptapuri for seven hundred years. The kingdom had never experienced war in its entire history.

But for Pashuspati, fate had other plans. He was the one destined to defend the kingdom of Saptapuri against the enemy at its threshold. What wouldn't he have given to end his reign in peace and hand over the crown to his son, Prince Chandrasekhara? This land had a rich and beautiful history, and he stood up with resolve to protect what was entrusted to him to govern.

He looked up at Maharaja Mahendragiri's portrait, Saptapuri's first ruler for guidance. His thoughts travelled to the powerful stone—the size of a sparrow's egg—kept in the Kabalishwar Vilas, protected by layers of security. That stone had brought the war to his very doorstep.

A sacred jewel

Millions of years ago, at the dawn of time, there rose from the ground a mountain range, large and most formidable. It rose so high that one couldn't tell where the peaks ended and the sky began. It was like a mysterious wall, cryptic and inscrutable. Called the Oundin range, it held the secrets of whatever lay beyond. Safely nestled within the range was the beautiful kingdom of Saptapuri, located at Sapta—the seventh mountain in the Oundin range. This mountain, known as the Soma Parvata, was a generous and giving guardian. Its slopes shimmered with abundance. Its forests were thick with minerals, herbs, and fruit trees. At the heart of the Soma Parvata, lay the mighty Pravasi Lake–a reservoir of purity and bounty.

The Oundin was protected on three sides by an escarpment that ended in a beautiful plateau.

Mahendragiri, the first Maharaja, was the leader of the Bhairava clan. He united all the small, warring tribes inhabiting a part of the Oundin mountain range. He promised to rule justly and bring peace, harmony and prosperity to all. True to his word, Mahendragiri established laws that fostered peace among the warring tribes. Subsequently, the Mahakal, Bhairava, Pingala, Chandrastara, Rudra, Kala and Anava tribes came together to form Saptapuri. The kingdom was the epitome of culture, prosperity and justice. Trade flourished in the kingdom, and its fame spread to the southern tip of the great lands, where the sky met the seas.

Amara—the capital city

Amara, the capital city of the kingdom, was built with chessboard-like precision and symmetry. An aerial view of the city would have resembled a chequered square locket studded with diamonds. The city consisted of ten blocks extending in each direction—north, south, east and west—bringing the total to forty divisions. The city centre was occupied by a large temple called the Smritisthala.

Amara had well-planned streets, an efficient drainage system and large granaries. The roads were laid in the north-south and east-west directions. It had bazaars and large stepwells for ritual cleansing. Each block was spread over a couple of acres and housed homes for all strata of society. There were two public baths in the northern block for women alone. There was one gurukul in the city where all children, including the king's, received their education. The city centre, which had the Smritisthala and several other public buildings, was situated at a higher level than the rest of the city. The pivotal point of the Smritisthala was made 25 feet elevated from its periphery. A network of wide roads and paths connected the city to the outside world.

The Adiparashakti fortress

Mahendragiri, the first ruler of Saptapuri, built a massive fortress by the lakefront to safeguard the city. The Adiparashakti fortress was an unassailable, irregular, rectangular structure spread over 6.25 km square. It was surrounded by a wide moat. The fortress itself was a mini kingdom and was built on seven levels. The highest or the seventh level housed the royal rooms, dining halls and a small temple for the royals. The next level had temples, gurukuls, open areas for play and six water tanks. The third, fourth and fifth levels had small quarters for the public. The lower-level housed stables, granaries and storage rooms for weapons. The last level was located underground and housed dungeons and prison cells.

The entire fortress had several turrets and 700 watch towers to keep vigil against enemy intrusion. There were eleven gateways, twenty back doors, three secret doors and some underground passages. The secret doors connected the fortress to the Smritisthala, the royal chambers in the palace, and to a safe hold in the forest through a network of independent and well-laid tunnels. None of the three tunnels had ever been used since they had been commissioned but they were all well maintained for security reasons.

The storage warehouses and reservoirs had been designed to store enough food, water and military supplies to survive a prolonged siege.

The outer walls of the fortress had a gate at each cardinal point. Additionally, small niches in the walls provided secure positions for archers to shoot arrows from. The height of the fortress walls ranged between forty and forty-five feet. The total length of the fortress walls was about ten kilometres in total.

Pataleshwar—An underground fort

Mahendragiri did not stop at building single safe and secure citadel. He also built an underground fort called Pataleshwar hidden deep in the Bhanre forest. Only people well conversant with the terrain could locate its entrance which was well camouflaged. On the northside of the fort, there was a sloped entrance resembling a slide. It let horses, wounded people and small carriages to enter and seek safety underground.

The Pataleshwar was a labyrinth of passages and rooms located deep below the earth's surface. This fort spanned a couple of kilometres and could shelter a small group of people for a limited time. Compared to the Adiparashakti fortress, it had fewer granaries, water tanks and houses.

A hidden tunnel snaked its way from the ancient sanctum of Pataleshwar, burrowing deep through the belly of the Bhanre forest, its path veiled by root and rock. If navigated correctly, it could lead to the formidable Adiparashakti Fortress—but the passage was not easy to conquer.

The long tunnel was interrupted by two concealed doors, each silently guarding the route ahead. Both stood side by side in a narrow alcove at the base of a stairwell, accessible only through a well-hidden trapdoor camouflaged among the forest's tangled undergrowth.

Neither door could be opened from within the tunnel itself—a deliberate failsafe, crafted to ensure that no invader who seized one stronghold could breach the other. The connection between Pataleshwar and Adiparashakti remained severed unless unlocked from the outside. When taking the tunnel from Pataleshwar, if the doors in the alcove had been unlocked, one would have to enter the alcove first and then squeeze into the connecting tunnel through the adjoining door to get to Adiparashakti.

Only one with knowledge of the secret trapdoor, buried

deep in Bhanre's shadowed heart, could access both locks to allow for passage between the two sites.

Saptapuri was planned so well that her subjects lived in peace and harmony. However, the kingdom guarded the greatest treasure the land had seen.

The Ajna Chakra

Saptapuri was the proud owner of the Ajna Chakra, a powerful and beautiful stone made of purple opal. Its shape resembled two lotus petals flanking a circle, which in turn contained an upside-down triangle whose points touched the circle's edge. The stone was the size of a sparrow's egg, radiating light that formed a halo around it. It was the most precious object south of the Oundin mountains. The king guarded the stone with a formidable force of trained warriors known as the Kabali.

The lore behind the stone was that it had been gifted by Lord Shiva to the head of the Mahakal clan in recognition of his devotion to the deity. It was said that the stone was crafted from the fire emanating from Shiva's third eye, and was thus named Ajna chakra. The stone was said to grant immortality, strength and power to whoever possessed it. If set into the headgear of its possessor, all of its powers would be transferred to the wearer. However, once depleted of all its powers, the stone would become nothing more than a beautiful ornament.

The king's council agreed that no man should wield such powers. The kings of Saptapuri knew the cost of being immortal. Their loved ones would be gone forever. Thus, the stone was safely locked away in the king's palace, with the Kabali guarding it.

The Kabali

Perhaps nobody had waged a war against the kingdom of Saptapuri for two reasons. One was the fabled power of the Ajna chakra, and the second was the unmatched skills, bravery and valour of the Kabali. They were elite soldiers, especially trained in martial arts and swordsmanship, with a singular mission: They were supposed to single-mindedly guard the Ajna chakra with their life. These warriors were selected at the age of ten after tough tests. They were enrolled in a separate *gurukul*, where they trained for up to twenty hours each day. They were taught to fight off hunger, sleep and carnal desires. They became fighting machines, equipped with the speed of a hunting tigress. They lived in the Kabalishwar Vilas, guarding the stone carefully.

The chief warrior of the Kabali was Anandamayi. She was the fiercest warrior anyone had ever seen and certainly the toughest chief the Kabali had known in a long time. People acknowledged that she was an extraordinary teacher, capable of training individuals to master the art of using weapons. Pashupati felt reassured knowing that Anandamayi was guarding the kingdom's greatest treasure against the raiders.

A threat to Saptapuri

Maharaja Pashupati's thoughts turned to the impending peril facing Saptapuri. Until now, he had only heard rumours about a barbaric raider called Moishan. People spoke about him in whispers. They said that he looked horrendous owing to all his evil deeds. His fair skin was marked with deep gashes and battle scars. His hair was long and curly, making his face look gigantic. It was said that his head had two peculiar, horn-like outgrowths. They protruded from his forehead, right at the hairline. These protrusions had earned him the moniker 'buffalo-demon'.

This monstrous warrior was at their doorstep now, intent upon destroying his beautiful kingdom to win the Ajna Chakra.

Pashupati wiped the beads of sweat from his brow and waited for his ministers and army chief to arrive. They had battle plans to discuss. The door opened, bringing in his two most trusted men—Gurupadaka, his chief minister, and Shankar, his army chief. They bowed before the king, and Pashupati beckoned them to join him at the centre table.

Gurupadaka put down some papers on the table and spread them out. They were maps of the kingdom and its neighbouring areas, marked in different coloured inks. It showed how far Moishan's army had infiltrated and which territories they had yet to conquer. The markings on the map showed that the evil raider had destroyed a significant portion of what had once been Saptapuri's neighbouring territories. Moishan's army was now stationed at Kirtiswaroopam, the ancient trade centre of the Oundin range. Little of Kirtiswaroopam was left after his attack. The destruction of this major trading hub had hit merchants in the region hard. Even, Saptapuri's economy was unstable. The people were restless, and achieving victory was crucial for Saptapuri and the nearby kingdoms.

Gurupadaka spoke in a heavy voice, 'Karnikapuri and Dwajasthapura have fallen. Of the five kingdoms that are our allies, we can only reach out to three for aid. I have sent emissaries to Maharajas Girijapati, Siddheshwara and Prajapati to inform them about the grave situation. I have highlighted the importance of strength in unity. Moishan will destroy our lands, even without the Ajna chakra. But with the stone's power, he will destroy all the kingdoms south of the Oundin mountains. Nothing can stop him. I hope the three kings respond favourably to our request for help.'

'What about the other two kingdoms?' questioned Shankar.

'After the *swayamvara*, I doubt Maharaja Krishnakanth of Karpura would want to deal with us. But we can try reaching out to Prince Samara of Sangha. He seems to be an honourable man. Pity that he lost his father at such a young age. He has not even been crowned king, and this trouble is upon us,' replied Pashupati.

'I can go personally to both kingdoms and make them understand our predicament,' said Gurupadaka. 'Your swayamvara was a long time ago. Let us hope King Krishnakanth has forgotten about it.'

'Meanwhile, Shankar, you must prepare for war regardless

of who is with us on the battlefield. Saptapuri has the largest army with the most valiant warriors. We must call out to every able-bodied man in Saptapuri. They must join our soldiers to fight the demon,' Gurupadaka stated.

'I may sound wishful, and this may seem like a desperate old man's rant. But have you considered the prophecy on the temple wall?' asked Pashupati. Though he had been sceptical about the legend in the past, he now sincerely hoped that this so-called prophecy had a ring of truth.

Nobody knew who had carved the strange figurines into the wall to convey a message or how long ago it was done. It was believed that Ma Durga guarded Saptapuri. The grace of Mahakaleshwar and the Goddess brought peace and prosperity to the lands. According to folklore, Ma Durga had appeared before the ancient tribes of the Soma Parvata and promised to protect them against future calamities. She would do this by appearing as one of her Navadurga (Durga's nine forms) avatars when the time came.

Gurupadaka stared hard at the Maharaja, unable to believe what he had just heard. Due to his profound respect for the king, he stayed calm. He said in a sombre tone, 'Ma Durga will come if and when she is truly needed by our people. But this is not the time to throw up our hands and wait for a miracle. This is a time to protect our people. We still believe in Lord Mahakaleshwar and Ma Durga, but this prophecy doesn't say when or how she will help us. We must put our minds together right now to find a practical way of confronting a demonic army.'

Pashupati was quick to agree with Gurupadaka's argument and reassured him. 'It was just a passing thought,' he said.

However, Shankar was a firm believer in this prophecy. He said, 'I know Ma Durga will come. She has quietly cared for our people for years. She will not let our faith go in vain. Although I am not sure when and how she will intervene to help us. So, I agree with Guru. We need to focus on finding a way to defend ourselves right now.'

Shankar then began filling them in on what he had learned about the enemy so far. He had stayed up all night putting together battle plans. He had met with the spies and had a lengthy discussion about the enemy's numbers and resources. According to one of the spies, Chennu, Moishan's army right now was stationed at Kirtiswaroopam, the trade centre, to gather supplies. He estimated that their forces comprised at least 49,000 soldiers. They were all light-skinned and had massive bodies and each of them was deformed in some way or the other. Some looked like bears, covered in hair. Some had twisted, hoof-like hands and feet, while others had huge lemon-sized growths all over their skin. They spoke in a tongue that was very harsh, sounding like the short barks of a wolf.

They were all dressed in short brown outfits. Cloth was wrapped around their lower bodies, reaching their calves. Their upper bodies were bare, but the spies had seen metal armour hanging around their tents, indicating they wore upper body armour. Their discarded boots were made of heavy leather and trimmed with soft fur. They also wore a strange assortment of colourful beads on their necks, wrists and ankles.

It was evident that they had travelled from a very cold place, making Saptapuri's tropical weather uncomfortable for them.

Shankar wondered where these warriors had come from. The Oundin mountains had long offered formidable protection to Saptapuri over the centuries. People of the region had never crossed this lofty range and were unaware of what lay on the other side.

Perhaps Moishan and his band of brigands had come from across the mountains. Shankar pondered what other horrors lay beyond the mountains of Oundin. He also considered the implications of losing the battle: it would set a dangerous precedent for all outsiders. Who knew how many others would cross over and challenge Saptapuri if they were defeated this time?

Shankar drew up some battle formations for his army. Their army of foot soldiers, cavalry, and archers was only 12,000-strong and also the largest among the seven kingdoms of the region. Even if they allied with some neighbouring kingdoms, their combined army would still be outnumbered by the demon's forces.

To make up for this handicap, Shankar would have to rely heavily on wit and clever tactics if they were to stand a chance of winning the battle. He planned to deploy elephants, cavalry, spearmen, and sword-wielding foot soldiers. Additionally, multiple rows of expert archers would be stationed on the higher planes and low-cut cliffs.

The tense discussion about the battle strategy was interrupted when the doors opened again. It was Anandamayi. She approached them in long strides and curtseyed before the king. The Maharaja nodded in acknowledgement.

Before anyone could say a word, she said, 'My king, please let the Kabali be a part of the battle. We are the best warriors you have in the entire kingdom. All our lives have been spent guarding the sacred stone. Today the stone and the kingdom require us to go to the battlefield to protect what we stand for. Please…'

Anandamayi's request was earnest. Her strong voice showed her deep concern. She looked at Shankar and Gurupadaka for support. Then she raised her hands in a desperate, questioning way.

'Anandamayi, you are partly right. Kabalis are the best warriors in the kingdom. This is precisely why you cannot leave the Ajna Chakra unguarded. The war is going to be fought over that stone. We cannot let our emotions take over and abandon our posts at such a crucial moment. You will best serve your kingdom and its people by guarding the Ajna chakra with your life,' responded Gurupadaka.

'I agree with the chief minister. We have an army that is fearless and valiant and trained for the battle. The Kabali, on the other hand, have been trained especially to guard the Ajna chakra. You are unique warriors. No one can replace you. The rest of us are expendable. Please do not abandon your post during this time of need,' said Shankar, his gentle voice almost pleading with Anandamayi.

'Fine then,' she said angrily and stomped away. But suddenly, she stopped in her tracks, turned towards Shankar and locked eyes with him—eyes which were full of anger and disappointment, a look only he noticed.

'I thought you were on my side. I expected you to understand, at least.' With that, she walked away as swiftly as she had come in.

Pashupati was a little surprised by Anadamayi's outburst, but at the same time, his heart filled with pride that he had such loyal subjects who were ready to lay down their lives for the sake of the kingdom. Tears welled up in his eyes. He turned towards the window, leaving Shankar and Guru to take care of the details. Looking down at the sprawling garden below, he saw Maharani Gautami picking flowers for her prayers. Seeing the queen so resplendent and composed, he wiped his eyes. He realized what a strong-willed woman Gautami was. Her resilience was evident during these troubled times, as she maintained her daily routine and not let her worries affect her people.

Maharaja Pashupati's wedding to Gautami had been a dramatic and unforgettable event that led to tensions between him and King Krishnakanth of Karpura. Hence, Gurupadaka feared that the latter would not ally with Saptapuri in this war against Moishan.

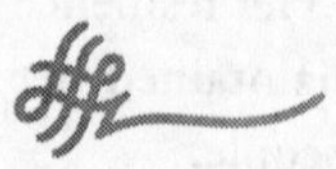

An unforgettable swayamvara

Thirty-seven years ago, Maharaja Vishvarup of Saptapuri received a royal invitation from Anagraha, a kingdom located south of the Oundin mountains. It requested Crown Prince Pashupati's presence at the swayamvara of Princess Gautami.

She was the eldest daughter of Maharaja Asmaka and Maharani Kanakavalli. In these lands, it was customary for the bride's father to set a tough challenge for the visiting princes. They had to demonstrate their bravery and intelligence to win the princess's hand. It was a matter of honour for any kingdom to have its prince prove his worth in front of all the other suitors. An invitation to a swayamvara was so coveted that all princes wanted one. But at the same time, they dreaded the prospect of competing against so many hot-headed rivals.

Prince Pashupati was sent to Asmaka with much pomp and show. Bringing home a bride was considered nothing short of winning a war. It was on this fateful day, sitting amongst many a worthy suitor, that Pashupati gave his heart to Gautami. She appeared nervous yet poised and radiant. She wore a dazzling pink saree, precious jewels and orange and white flowers in her braid. She smiled at him when their eyes met, just as she had done to acknowledge each prince present at the gathering.

Raja Asmaka stood up. He welcomed the princes warmly and thanked them for coming to Anagraha. He then laid out the terms of the challenge. The princess's favourite bird, the Neelkant, had to be caught and brought back alive and unharmed before dusk. Although the bird was not rare, the clause requiring it to be brought back alive posed a significant challenge for the princes, making the task quite difficult. The king announced that if there were multiple winners by dusk, a tiebreaker would take place the following day.

All the princes set out into the forest beyond Anagraha, armed and equipped with the necessary tools. The forest was densely populated with sal, wood apple (*bel*), ebony, bamboo and mahua trees. These were interspersed with large numbers of teak trees, their massive leaves swaying in the gentle breeze. The forest floor was damp from the previous night's rain, and the monsoon had brought out swarms of winged termites. Pashupati waded through shrubs in the forest, periodically flicking the insects off his neck and forearms. Every now and then, he would run into another suitor who, like him, had had no luck so far. It was nearing dusk, and darkness slowly began to take hold, spreading her wings over the steely-grey clouds. The competition would be called off soon, and no winner had been announced as yet.

Just as Pashupati thought he would return empty-handed, he spotted the Neelkant. It was perched on a low branch, its head buried in a crevice of the tree. The bird seemed busy digging out termites and feasting on them. Pashupati stopped dead in his tracks. He stood there, breathless, watching the tiny bird. He wondered if he could catch it without hurting it. The very next second, the bird sensed his presence and flew up to a higher branch of the tree. Pashupati pulled out crumbs of food from his pocket, remnants of the frugal lunch he had had earlier in the day. He held his hand out and whistled to the bird. It looked at him, cocked its head to the right as if it were mocking him, and chirped. And then, suddenly, it flew right down and sat on the palm of his hand. Pashupati could not believe his luck. Hardly daring to breathe, he gently cradled the bird in his other hand. He then placed her in a small, makeshift cage he had prepared. The bird looked up at him from the cage and chirped again, but it did not appear distressed. Pashupati looked towards the sky, thanking the gods above, and began his trek back to town.

As Pashupati entered the palace triumphantly, he saw that Prince Krishnakanth of Karpura had also captured the bird alive. He joined Pashupati in front of the gathering before the king. King Asmaka congratulated both princes, relieved them of the birds, and recommended that they go to their chambers to freshen up before dinner. He announced that a tiebreaker would be arranged for the following morning.

Morning came, bringing news that the tiebreaker would be an archery event. The losing princes joined the king, queen and princesses as spectators. Pashupati and Krishnakanth had taken centre stage, standing with their backs to each other. Each prince faced a large bel tree, and their target was to bring down as much fruit as possible in five minutes. At the sound of the conch, both princes began shooting. They went on relentlessly, despite the fact that shooting arrows in succession was an arduous task. Their hands began to ache, but the princes only stopped when the conch blew again to signal the end of the challenge. They turned around to see how the other man had performed. Pashupati could see that Krishnakanth by now had begun to hate him. He stared at Pashupati with dagger-like eyes and a venomous expression. By some mischief of God, both princes had shot down the same number of fruits. King Asmaka again congratulated both princes and welcomed them back to the palace.

Princess Gautami was waiting, dressed in a shade of orange that resembled the softest rays of the evening sun. A maiden holding garlands of beautiful red and white flowers stood beside her. Pashupati's eyes wandered around a bit and then settled on Gautami. She looked away at once. Pashupati gazed at her beautiful face. He wondered what would happen next. Would there be another test that he had to clear to win Gautami's hand?

Just then, King Asmaka cleared his throat and spoke: 'Let us congratulate both princes. They have shown honour, strength and spirit over the last two days. They have both done exceedingly well, and each one deserves the hand of my daughter Gautami. Unfortunately, that is not possible. I am leaving it up to my daughter to choose her groom. She will decide which of the two princes is the best match for her.'

Krishnakanth opened his mouth to say something but thought better of it and remained silent. The king took both princes by the hand and led them to the centre stage. All eyes were upon the princess now. Who would she choose between the two princes?

Pashupati could feel his heart beating so hard that he was afraid that everyone around him could hear it. He thought that Princess Gautami was an exceptionally beautiful woman. He had also heard of her remarkable skills with both the sword and the bow. Word had it that her intelligence and wit were unparalleled. It would be a matter of honour for him to have her as his future queen.

Both men waited, looking at the princess. Meanwhile,

the other princes, outshone by Pashupathi and Krishnakanth, wondered which of these two valiant men would emerge victorious. The princess approached the two men and stopped two feet away. She looked at Pashupati, who managed a half smile. She then cast her gaze on Krishnakanth. Pashupati didn't dare look but could feel the tension in the air. She continued to study Krishnakanth for a minute longer. Then she pivoted and placed the garland around Pashupati's neck. The hall erupted in thunderous applause, and some of the courtiers began to chant, 'Hail the crown prince of Saptapuri, Rajkumar Pashupati, the chosen suitor of Princess Gautami.'

Krishnakanth did not wait another moment and turned to leave. His blood boiled, and he seethed under the weight of his perceived humiliation. As he walked past the crowd, he felt their eyes burning into his skin.

After Pashupati had exchanged garlands with Gautami, they turned to the court for blessings. Pashupati saw Krishnakanth's back in the distance. Just as Krishnakanth was about to exit the hall, he turned. He locked eyes with Pashupati and partially drew his sword. Then he slammed it back in. It was a message: 'I will repay this humiliation.'

Gautami played every role of hers to perfection. She was a devout maharani to her subjects. She was a bold and fierce mother, loving and protective of her son, yet uncompromising where his education was concerned. She was the best wife a king could ask for. She helped Pashupati with state affairs, at times making tough decisions that even he was surprised by. She took a personal interest in her son Chandrasekhara's schooling and weapon training. She never backed down from an opinion out of fear and always valued integrity above every other virtue. Pashupati was blessed to have Gautami by his side during these challenging times, when the very existence of Saptapuri was at stake. He made a mental note to have her join the war room discussions once she completed her tasks.

To the battlefield

'Maharaja, what do you think?' said a voice, snapping Pashupati out of his reverie. It was Shankar pointing at a drawing on his board, scrutinizing the cogency of the formation in question.

'We should regroup with all the important members in the palace. Set up the meeting. Request Maharani Gautami, Rajkumar Chandrasekhara, Rajguru Dhumbaka, Acharya Veni, Vaidya Vidhushi, and Anandamayi to join us. We will need all ideas and hands on deck to come up with a sound plan.'

The war council spent three whole days in the war room, strategizing for worst-case scenarios both on and off the battlefield. From time to time, some members left to complete tasks assigned to them, while spies would occasionally arrive with news of enemy movements.

Anandamayi was still miffed about the fact that she and the other Kabali warriors were not allowed to join the battle. Though she was an active part of the discussions, it was obvious to everyone that she was angry and was avoiding Shankar. She barely looked at him over the three days and didn't address him directly, even when she had something to say. Perturbed by her behaviour, Vidhushi pulled Anandamayi aside for a private chat.

'What is going on with you Anandamayi? Your behaviour

is marring the spotless reputation you have built so far. You are a fiery warrior chief. What makes you act this way?' she questioned.

'Sister, it's difficult to explain how I'm feeling right now. I spent all my childhood training to fight without food, sleep or even normal human contact. I have kept away from intimate relationships, friendship or love. I am, to this day, very emotionally detached even from my brother and parents. But with Shankar, it is different. His kindness and benevolence are beyond comparison, and he is both gentle and fierce at the same time. He is both beautiful and gruesome when he fights, showing perfection even in all his imperfections. He has always been a genuine advisor and friend since I became the chief of Kabalis. I fear that if I do not go to the battlefield with him, I may never get a chance to see him again, tell him how I feel or say what I want to say.'

'Anandamayi, your words express the deep fear that many of us are feeling but are afraid to voice. We are all tormented by the thought of losing a loved one in the impending war. All we can do is have faith in our abilities and put our best foot forward. The rest is up to Lord Mahakaleshwar and Ma Durga. You have trained all your life to guard the Ajna Chakra. Do you want cause irreparable loss by abandoning your duty at this critical hour? What you wish to tell Shankar can wait. I suspect he is already aware of how you feel. Don't think that he doesn't notice things. Sometimes, I believe, he knows all and sees all. If you still feel the same after the threat passes, you will have all the time in the world to express your feelings. Now is not that time. Be the warrior you were meant to be.'

Just then, Gurupadaka returned from visiting both the

neighbouring kingdoms. With him was the best surprise that Saptapuri could have asked for.

The entire room was stunned upon seeing their new guest. Pashupati rushed to his guest and embraced him with warmth. 'I never thought Karpura would stand by us in our time of need. Not in my wildest dreams did I expect you here, Raja Krishnakanth.'

'Let bygones be bygones, Maharaja Pashupati. I believe that both of us behaved with utmost honour and chivalry that day, and I must say the best man won. I trust Maharani Gautami is in good health as we speak.'

'That I am, sir,' said Gautami, joining her husband's side. 'We welcome you to the great land of Saptapuri and apologize that your welcome couldn't be a grander affair in these perilous times.'

'Let us not waste precious time on formalities, my queen. I am told that there is much to be done,' Krishnakanth said respectfully.

That evening, Gurupadaka reported more unwelcome news than good, which was both disappointing and a setback for the war preparations.

King Siddheshwara of Sahasrara, the southernmost kingdom in the Oundin range, had refused to help. He stated that Saptapuri should fight its own battles and that they did not want to die protecting Saptapuri's treasure. Similar sentiments had been expressed by Kings Girijapati and Prajapati of the twin kingdoms of Dhupghar and Rupghar.

Thankfully, Crown Prince Samara of Sangha had pledged his support to Saptapuri. Additionally, news had also come from Maharani Gautami's homeland, Anagraha. Although her father had passed away long ago, her brother Grehan had agreed to lend his troops to Saptapuri.

With only a few allies joining the war effort, Shankar realized that their numbers were underwhelming compared to the buffalo-demon's army.

'They outnumber us by a margin of 20,000 soldiers. Also, spies have informed us that Moishan's army is equipped with weapons never seen before. We are going up against a mighty barbarian and we need tenacity, wit and valour to overcome this predicament.'

On the third evening, it was decided that an emissary would be sent to Kirtiswaroopam. On behalf of Saptapuri and its allies, the messenger would request Moishan—who was camped there—to call off the war and state his demands. Everyone agreed that if Moishan acceded to their request, there would be no cause for concern. If not, an attack would be launched five days after the messenger's return. All visiting kings, troops and cavalry will be given food and shelter and taken care of until then.

Maharani Gautami and her brother Raja Grehan were to oversee the housing and other facilities for soldiers and kings from other kingdoms. Large campsites were organized outside the city limits, close to the battleground.

Vidhushi and her team of doctors prepared herbs, ointments, syrups and lotions to heal the sick and wounded. They checked their supply of bandages and operating tools in case surgeries needed to be performed.

Shankar and Chandrasekhara gathered the *senapati*s or generals of all armies and briefed them on the battle plans, formations and tactics.

All that was left to do was wait for news from their messenger now. The dignitaries from visiting kingdoms joined the royal table for lunch the next day. It was a sombre affair. Their meal was interrupted when Shankar hurriedly entered the dining room and walked towards the king with some urgency. He whispered something in Pashupati's ear and the king at once excused himself from the table. The other dignitaries paused their meal, insisting they would resume when the Maharaja returned to the table.

'The situation is a bit grave. Please finish your meal and join us in the war room as soon as you can. I will have to excuse myself for now,' the king said, before leaving the room with Shankar close at his heels.

They mounted their horses and rode to the medical centre which was further away from the palace grounds. When he entered the facility, Pashupati cringed and closed his eyes. The sight in front of him was the last thing he had expected to see. On the bed lay the almost lifeless form of Surma, the messenger. He was bloodied and wounded; his left arm, three toes and an eye were missing. His face was swollen beyond recognition, and the only identifying feature was a distinctive tattoo of the Saptapuri emblem on his right wrist.

Vidhushi assured Pashupati that Surma was being taken care of. The Maharaja walked out of the medical facility, motioning to Shankar to follow.

'Make sure that he is taken care of well. Look out for his family and assure them of our support and goodwill. We will launch an attack on Kirtiswaroopam in two days. Ready your troops for battle. If it is a war he wants, he will get it,' he spat in anger.

News about Surma's condition spread like wildfire, and it struck terror into the hearts of the soldiers. If a messenger was treated in such a barbaric manner, what would happen to them on the battlefield? Shankar seemed to have his job cut out for him. His inspiring speeches failed to convince his soldiers, and they appeared defeated even before the battle began. They prepared for the combat with fear in their hearts. Shankar realized that with such low spirits running through his troops, they were sure to be wiped out on the battlefield. He thought long and hard about the battle strategy. He felt that initiating the attack on Moishan's army was folly. Seeking guidance, he decided to share his thoughts with Gurupadaka, his good friend and mentor.

'Guru, getting to Kirtiswaroopam by foot is a three-day march. The men would be tired and sore when they reach there they would be in no shape to battle a demon army. Their morale is already down and making them march to a battle will sap their remaining strength. I believe we should be ready for the battle but let Moishan bring the battle to us. What do you say?'

'Son, you know that I am going to agree with you. Your clarity of thought and your earnest beliefs always make me feel like I am conversing with Lord Mahadev. You are like a mirror, reflecting his thoughts. Should you be second-guessing your decisions? I think not. You do not need my validation for this. Let us share your thoughts with the Maharaja.'

Shankar embraced Gurupadaka tightly. 'You think very highly of me, sir. I hope I remain worthy of it always.'

The war council was convened, and Shankar proposed his revised strategy—to wait for the enemy to make their move instead of launching an attack first.

'But we could be sitting at the edge of the battlefield for weeks. The anxiety alone will kill us faster than the battle itself,' said an agitated Pashupati. He had aged rapidly over the last three weeks, but was determined to see things through to their end. It seemed that he wanted to avenge all the death, destruction and mutilation in the neighbouring territories.

'I completely agree with Shankar,' said Krishnakanth. 'We

will fight with everything we have got. But why go looking for a fight? We should wait for it to come to us.'

'Maharaja, Moishan is after the Ajna Chakra. He is not going to be sitting around for long. The battle will come to us, and it will come quick. Let us boost our soldiers' morale by staying on familiar ground.' Gautami knew how to persuade Pashupati and make him see the rationale behind the plan.

It was agreed, then, that they would prepare and wait. The wait wasn't very long. The next evening, the kingdom's spies brought news that Moishan's army was on the move and rapidly marching towards Amara.

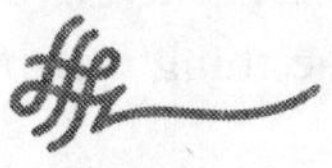

The stranger in the battlefield

It was the first day after the new moon in the sixth month of the *Rakthakshi Samvatsara* (the 58th year in a 60-year Hindu calendar). The dawn brought with it the greatest battle that Saptapuri had ever had to fight yet. The combined armies of Samara, Karpura, Anagraha and Saptapuri stood facing a sea of warriors painted in black. Never had one seen such a formidable force. Shankar was right in calling it the demon army.

'Today is a day that will go down in history as a memorable one,' Shankar's voice boomed.

'We stand between the demons and the Ajna Chakra. We will fight as long as it takes and as hard as needed. We defend a treasure so valuable that if we fail, there will be no kingdom to return to. We will fight till there is no man left to defend our walls. Or we will fight until there is no man left in their ranks to stand against us. We will fight today for our people, for peace and all of humanity. May Mahakaleshwar stand with us today. Hara, Hara!'

'Hara, Hara,' came the resounding reply from the soldiers. Shankar had spoken to every soldier over the last few days to lift their spirits and bolster their determination. His battlefield speech made everybody's hair stand on end. They felt energized and charged. Each soldier felt that if there was one thing worth laying down his life for, it was *Senapati* Shankar.

'Hara, Hara, repeated Shankar. And this time, all the kings, princes and ministers joined him.

None from the king's army had yet spotted Moishan. His army was led by gruesome-looking generals.

The loud sound of a bugle reverberated through the air, and with it, both armies charged forward, crashing into each other's lines. The Buffalo Demon's army was like an unending wave of soldiers.

Pashupati and Raja Krishnakanth were on elephant backs, using their exceptional archery skills and the advantage of height to rain arrows upon the demon army. Pashupati was goading his mahout to use the strength of the elephant to crush as many enemy soldiers as possible. Princes Chandrasekhara and Samara and King Grehan had chosen to be on horseback amidst the soldiers.

Shankar looked at his warriors with pride as they threw themselves into the fight. Soon, he got into a duel with a heavyset, ogre-like man. Even though he was seated on a horse, Shankar realized that his enemy's head almost came up to his chest. The ogre had a sword, its width thrice that of Shankar's. Its sharp edge curved in a concave manner, and the blunt end was lined with razor sharp teeth. It was a weapon like nothing Shankar had ever seen before.

With one thrust of his forearm, the gigantic man pushed Shankar off his horse and pinned him to the ground. Shankar's head was inches from the edge of the thick, curved blade. He sharply brought his sword in between and blocked the weapon from slitting his throat. His arms were shivering from the sheer effort it took to keep the massive weapon and its equally massive wielder away.

With one solid effort, Shankar pushed up from his waist. Simultaneously, he moved his upper body forward, thrusting his chest into his own sword, using its force to push the enemy's blade away while attempting to kick him in the groin. He managed to push the beast off balance for a second. Using this time, he tucked his arms and rolled over just as the man regained his balance and aimed another blow. The huge cutter landed on the earth where Shankar's head had been moments before. Shankar deftly jumped back onto his feet and swung his blade at his enemy. The hefty sword swung back at him, dislodging Shankar's sword from his hand. Shankar nimbly bent down, picked up a spear from a fallen soldier, and drove it into the tall, gigantic mass bearing down on him. He let the weight of the man do the rest as the body keeled over, driving the spear deeper into the mass of flesh. Shankar picked up his fallen sword and turned to find his horse.

Meanwhile, Krishnakanth was under heavy attack from his opponents as well. Two heavyset, troll-sized men were hacking at the legs of his elephant. The elephant trumpeted in pain and started swaying wildly. Krishnakanth tried his best to shoot at the enemy but was unable to take proper aim. At the same time, the elephant was trying to kick its attackers; it lifted its forelegs high into the air, landing on one of the men. Seeing his mate crushed under the feet of the animal, the other man backed away. However, the elephant's action unhinged the basket in which Krishnakanth sat. He fell out and hit the ground hard. Before he could pick himself up, a spear came flying towards him but missed its mark. And Krishnakanth could thank Pashupati for that, because even before the spearman could properly aim, an arrow had landed in his throat, finishing him off. Krishnakanth looked up to see Pashupati nodding at him. Krishnakanth nodded back and marched forward, picking up the sword of the fallen enemy.

Amid the clanking of swords, the pounding of feet and the thundering of hooves on the ground, the heart-wrenching cries of nameless soldiers who were mercilessly being stabbed and killed rent the air. So many of them had fallen that the earth was burdened by their weight, soaking in their blood until the sky grew dark and both armies withdrew for the day.

The allied forces picked up their dead and gave them an honourable farewell, and carried their wounded to medical camps for treatment.

That evening, Pashupati's tent was bustling with activity as the leaders discussed the next course of action. The numbers in their army had dwindled steadily, while the enemy appeared to have lost just a handful. The fact that Moishan had not been sighted confused everyone. Was he afraid to face the brave warriors of the allied forces or did he think his lieutenants were sufficient to handle such a meek force?

In light of the unfolding situation, it was agreed that the residents of Amara, along with the Ajna Chakra and the trusted Kabali, needed to be shifted to the Adiparashakti fortress. The wounded had to be nursed back to health. The maharani and other women were tirelessly working to take care of the injured under Vidhushi's supervision, while the latter was performing surgeries on the gravely wounded patients.

The second day of battle was no different from the first. By dusk, they were counting their losses and wondering if they could sustain the battle any longer. Battle tactics were discussed and reviewed threadbare until they no longer made sense. Shankar proposed new formations for the remaining troops, and everyone agreed to them for lack of other options.

On the third day, when the sun was directly overhead and at its fiercest, something unexpected occurred on the battlefield. However, it was something they had been hoping and praying for. One amongst them all, Shankar, strongly believed that it was destined to happen, though even he wasn't sure when and how it would occur.

The air in the middle of the battlefield became opaque and began blazing like a ring of fire. The centre was filled with thick smoke. Soldiers from both sides were thrown off their feet and knocked unconscious. Shankar, who was fighting a few meters away, sensed that this was no ordinary occurrence. With one swift move of his sword, he slit the throat of his opponent and manoeuvred his horse in the direction of the divine elliptical shape.

Landing in a nightmare!

Gauri hit the ground hard, dust rising all around her. Still reeling under the effect of being engulfed by smoke, she went momentarily blank. An eerie silence enveloped her.

As she tried to stand up slowly, she heard the sounds of clanking metal and heavy footsteps all around her. She wiped the dust off her eyes as they adjusted to her new surroundings. And just in time too!

She saw a horse galloping towards her at full speed. Just as quickly as Gauri had regained her footing, she lost it again. She fell and froze in the path of the speeding animal, her eyes locked on the rider. Though paralyzed with fear, Gauri's keen sight drank in the details.

He was an unusually tall soldier, fully armoured and his head was covered by a helmet. On his chest, right in the middle of his armour, was a crest set in a bright orange circle. It had a beautiful trident with a *damroo* (a pellet drum that symbolizes a connection with Lord Shiva), standing upright. At the base of the trident knelt a host of people, offering water.

Staring at her death as it rode towards her, she took a deep breath and shut her eyes. Suddenly, a strong hand grabbed her waist. Her eyes flew open to find the horse's flank right next to her face, its mane of hair whipping her cheek. The rider had deftly hoisted her onto the horseback and continued to ride on.

Gauri couldn't believe what was happening. She pinched herself, still dazed by it all. The pinch hurt, but not as much as her head, which ached with disbelief. Finally, she had time to absorb her surroundings. She was on a battlefield, with fierce warriors fighting to the death.

The soldier silently rode on. He skilfully avoided the foot soldiers as he steered his horse away from the battlefield. Gauri looked at others on the battlefield and wondered if she had lost her mind. What was happening to her? How did she get from being in a laboratory one moment to a battlefield the next? She struggled to rationalize the situation, but there seemed to be no logical explanation.

For a moment, Gauri's thoughts wandered to the battlefield. She wondered why the battle was being fought and between whom it was being fought.

However, her focus quickly shifted back to herself. Was she hallucinating? Did her brain get damaged when the beaker exploded? But she couldn't be dreaming or hallucinating all of this. For one, the horse she was riding felt so real. So did all the terrible noises rising from the field around her.

This realization scared Gauri and she began praying to get out of this nightmare alive. Gauri's mystery rescuer had not spoken at all. He nimbly avoided arrows, spears and enemy soldiers. Just as she thought they'd made it to the battle's edge, an arrow flew at her from the left. It struck her upper arm, just below the shoulder, piercing deep into her skin. Blood spurted out, flecks flying towards her face, dotting her cheeks and hair. She screamed in pain.

'Hold on to me Devi,' said the mystery man, 'I will get you to safety.'

In immense pain, Gauri obeyed meekly. She held on to the rider with her right arm as he spurred his horse on with a gentle kick. Soon, they left the battleground and entered a thick forested area with dense trees. The path was rough with rocks and boulders strewn around and the trees formed a dense canopy, almost blocking the sun out.

Gauri was drained by the excruciating pain and loss of blood and could barely think. Slowly, her eyes began to blur, and her hand was unable to grip her saviour anymore. Her fingers slipped. She lost her hold and suddenly, everything went dark.

Thump! She passed out and fell off the horse onto the forest floor.

When Gauri awoke, she found herself in a small dimly lit room. She could feel a gentle breeze coming from somewhere. A sliver of sunlight streamed through a small, square window in the left upper corner of the ceiling. Her bed was made of heavily carved wood and adorned with silken sheets. Beyond the bed, she saw silk drapes that hung from the ceiling to the floor. A gentle breeze caused slight ripples in the curtain, resembling blue waters stirred by light wind.

Gauri looked down at her wounded arm and saw that it was wrapped in bandages. She couldn't feel the pain anymore—one less thing to worry about for the moment. She was startled to discover that she was dressed in the most bizarre attire ever. She wore a saree, draped like ancient warriors. A blouse, knotted at her back, left her shoulders and forearms bare, just as in her dreams. A sudden clenching in her stomach brought a wave of despair. She tried to make sense of her surroundings.

Her thoughts were interrupted by the sound of footsteps. Gauri rose from the bed just as a lady dressed similarly entered the room. 'Please don't stand up Devi, your body requires rest,' she said gently.

'But,' began a defiant Gauri.

'I would listen to the *rajvaidya* if I were you,' said a voice that Gauri recognized as that of the rider who had rescued her. She was curious to see the face of the man who had saved her. A mix of fear and excitement gripped her. It was like a fangirl awaiting her favourite hero's entrance in a movie.

The curtains parted, revealing the most handsome man Gauri had ever seen. He was tall, at least six feet in height, and had a beautiful face with high cheekbones and an angular jawline. His broad forehead bore the *tripundra*—three horizontal lines of ash with a red dot in the centre. His long hair fell to his neck, just below his ears. His eyes looked large and compassionate. His aura was calm and meditative, as was his presence.

Gauri's eyes were drawn to his broad chest, partially covered by a yellow sash draped across his torso, running from his left shoulder and tucked into the right side of his waistband. His dhoti was pleated neatly in the front and held at the waist by a *mekhela*, an ornamental belt. Beneath the sash, the sacred thread or the *upavita* was partially visible. The man had the physique of a well-built warrior. When he smiled at Gauri, a dimple appeared in his left cheek, making him look both knowing and innocent.

'I hope our hospitality meets your expectations while you are here. I am Shankar, the chief of the armed forces of the kingdom of Saptapuri. Your arrival has left some of our people flummoxed. However, many of us had been waiting for your arrival. We will move you to your suite as soon as Vidhushi certifies that you are fit to be moved.'

'I'm sorry! Did you anticipate my arrival? You knew I would

come here?' she asked, sounding both confused and desperate. She looked at him pleadingly; she wanted answers.

'Devi,' began Shankar, but he was rudely interrupted by a confused and infuriated Gauri. 'I am Gauri. Please call me that.'

Shankar beamed like a thousand suns and nodded, as if he had expected her name to be Gauri. 'Interesting,' he quipped.

'What's interesting? Could you please stop with the riddles and tell me where I am and what is going on here?'

'Gauri, you are in the illustrious kingdom of Saptapuri. Our kingdom comprises seven clans led by the glorious King Pashupati. Our home is in great danger. A demonic warrior, Moishan, threatens to destroy us. The battle from which you were removed has cost us heavily. Those of us who went to battle rode into the forest safehold and the rest of our kingdom has been moved into our Adiparashakti fortress by the lakeside. The covert operation had been planned and executed by our leaders soon after the enemy arrived at our borders. We plan to join the rest of our army at the Adiparashakti fortress and fight back soon.'

'An ancient prophecy, carved into our temple walls, foretold your coming. It was long before our time,' he sighed, his chest rising and falling with his breath.

'Our kingdom is situated at the centre of the Soma Parvata in the Oundin range of mountains. We are surrounded by hills on three sides, with the great Lake Pravasi running on the eastern side of the kingdom. At the mouth of the lake, where it narrows to meet the river Narmada, we have a cave temple. The temple enshrines our deity Lord Mahakaleshwar and his consort Devi Durga. The temple is as ancient as our kingdom and was built by our first king, Maharaja Mahendragiri. But the temple's back wall is part of the hill behind it and was not built by our king.'

'The wise men of the Mahakal tribe, the oldest in this region, say that this wall has existed for thousands of years, long before our kingdom emerged. On this wall are a series of carvings that illustrate a story. Legends say that these etchings foretell a time of great peril, and the land during that time will need much more than the protection offered by our sacred mountains and brave warriors. It depicts a goddess who will reclaim the lands from the demons by slaying them. It is a tale of troubled times. The murals speak of an elliptical gateway, as bright as the sun. Through this portal, a goddess from another world will come to purge our lands of the demons and save our people.'

'That morning, on the battlefield, my fellow warriors and I saw this exact miracle. The air became thick and seemed to part, creating a blazing, elliptical opening. As I stood watching this spectacle, the opening grew brighter and brighter, as if the sun god himself had descended to Earth. But the blazing fire only formed a ring around the oval gateway, and its centre was dark and filled with crimson smoke. And just as suddenly as it appeared, the ring began to close. As the smoke cleared, you fell through it and landed on the battlefield.

The soldiers around you froze, just as shocked as you were. The ones far from the scene were oblivious to the happenings and continued to fight the enemy. This gave me the chance to ride forward and pick you up. And now, here we are, deep in the mountain range, at one of our underground safe locations.'

When Shankar stopped speaking, the room went quiet. There was air was so thick with tension that nobody dared to speak. Vidhushi, the royal doctor, was barely breathing. She waited for Gauri to react.

Gowri frowned.

'That is the most absurd thing I've ever heard,' she said,

ever so softly, breaking the silence. 'I am here because of a clumsy lab accident and not to fulfil any prophecy of yours. I am no goddess, and I am no warrior. You have your hopes pinned on the wrong woman, and I need to find a way back to my own world.'

Shankar opened his mouth to respond. But he quickly closed it when Vidhushi touched his forearm, her face grim and motherly. Shankar never questioned his sister, especially if it concerned her patient.

'I suggest that you rest for a while. If you have to figure out a way back to your land, you will need strength of body and mind to do it. We will stay out of your way till you decide how you would like to go ahead,' said Vidhushi.

She yanked Shankar's hand and marched him out of the room. Just beyond the door, Gauri heard their footsteps halt.

'Why didn't you let me convince her?' an agitated Shankar hissed.

'Do you want to wear her thin by your arguments, adding to her existing wounds and worries?' Vidhushi's tone was very matter of fact. 'Our ancient texts state, "*Sva bhavo vijayati iti shauryam*" (True heroism is to conquer your own nature). Give her time. Accepting who she is, is the first step towards fulfilling her purpose.'

As their footsteps faded, silence fell. Gauri was left alone to think.

Gauri and the royals

The underground safe hold was well planned. Gauri had spent the first three to four days after her recovery roaming around, exploring different rooms. She avoided people as much as she could. Her stomach burned with anxiety; she feared everyone she met would ask her to save or rescue them. Some of the people she passed in the corridors looked at her with such reverence in their eyes that it irritated her.

'They are all ridiculous,' she thought to herself. 'I am a research scientist. I am not going to rescue anyone or save the land from trouble.'

She had decided that she would keep her head down, stay out of trouble and keep trying to find a way back home. Much to her horror, she realized that she had travelled back in time by several eras to a war-torn ancient kingdom. Additionally, she was displaced geographically within this entire space-time continuum. It was too much to take, and the scientist in her found it hard to believe this could actually happen.

Gauri refused to join everyone in the dinner hall for meals. Instead, she ate her meals in her small but spacious room in the underground fort. This afternoon, as she looked down at her plate, she felt completely disconnected. She craved for something delicious. What wouldn't she give to have a pizza, a burrito or even her mother's aromatic rice and *rasam*? Amma's 'world-famous rasam' was Gauri's comfort food. A momentary smile crossed her lips as she pictured her mother walking around pompously asking relatives, 'How is the rasam, how is the rasam?' The relatives, in turn, cooed about how this was the best-tasting rasam in all of Bengaluru. Amma would then pretend to pat herself on the back.

Suddenly, she missed home more than ever. It felt like she was drowning. She couldn't breathe, and a sharp pain tore through her lungs. She gasped for breath, as if she was flailing beneath deep dark waters.

Bam! The door to her room burst open. She felt as if someone had switched on the lights in her head, and she came tumbling back to her painful reality.

It was Vidhushi, who came regularly to check on her. It had been a week since the arrow had pierced her arm. While the wound had healed, the arm was still sore, and she couldn't lift it or do much else with it. Gauri feigned a smile as Vidhushi walked in.

'You haven't touched your food, Gauri. Don't you like it? Please tell us if we can have the kitchen prepare something to your liking. We will do everything we can for you. But remember that our resources are limited and our supplies are running thin since yesterday.'

'What kind of an offer was that?' thought Gauri. Vidhushi was being hospitable but, in the same breath, also bluntly telling her about the meagre supplies. 'Weird lady,' she thought. From what she had seen over the last week, Vidhushi seemed like a loving, caring and tender person. Yet, she could also be stern, and her approach to things was rather blunt. She looked even more tired and harrowed than the last time she had visited her.

Gauri wanted to enquire if things were fine, but she was afraid of what she might hear and what they might expect from her. So, she just nodded her head in a manner that conveyed a no.

'I am fine, thank you. I just don't want to eat right now,' she said.

'Your arm has healed well. However, you need to start functional training to regain its flexibility and full use. Shankar excels in both teaching the different *kriya*s that accelerate healing and promote better health. He will see you at dawn tomorrow, so you can begin your training.' This sounded more like an order. She wasn't asking Gauri if she would like to learn; she was telling Gauri to learn. For a moment, a flash of anger crossed Gauri's face.

'Oh, I forgot! The royal family would be coming down to meet you this evening, sometime before dusk,' she said.

The anger was at once replaced by despair. Gauri did not want to meet the royals; it would be too much pressure to handle. She wasn't one of them. She wasn't who they wanted her to be. She couldn't be. Gauri had the urge to just run away. But where would she go? How could she go? The thoughts swimming in her head became overwhelming, and Gauri began to cry as soon as Vidhushi left. She was sobbing silently into the soft pillow when there was a knock on the door. She quickly wiped her eyes, straightened her clothes and looked up. It was Shankar.

Every time she saw him, he took her breath away. Gauri, despite not wanting to, always enjoyed Shankar's visits. They were brief, enquiring, and usually peppered with humour. He made light of the grave situation and the crazy expectations of his people.

Shankar smiled at her.

'How are you feeling today? My sister tells me that you have not eaten your food. I understand how you must be feeling. You're longing to find your way back. This is clear from your face as well as your behaviour. You are avoiding all human contact out of fear that we would get you mixed up in our messy business.'

Gauri nodded.

'Don't be afraid. Nobody here will ask you to do anything that you are not ready for. I have spoken to the Maharaja and explained your predicament to him. He is aware that you are from another world and do not consider yourself to be the warrior goddess of our prophecy. We all respect your wishes and will do our best to help you find your way back. But in the meantime, I would ask that you start talking to people. Join us for meals and have normal interactions, lest you get lost in the depths of your mind.'

Again, Gauri nodded. Why did she feel so compelled to agree with everything Shankar said? It was as if he held her in a hypnotic sway.

'I will teach you some kriyas and meditation practices to accelerate your healing and cleanse your aura. Vidhushi has given me strict orders about that. Could you please meet me in the clearing on the forest floor above just before daybreak tomorrow?"

She nodded. Shankar turned to go. 'Wait,' came a very timid voice.

Shankar was surprised. This was the first time the dusky, ethereal beauty had spoken to him after her fiery outburst. He spun around and looked at her. She looked like a frightened, lost child. He wanted to embrace her, kiss her forehead and tell her that everything was going to be all right. Instead, he just smiled and said, 'Yes, Gauri?'

'The royal family is coming to see me this evening. I have never met kings and queens before. I am not sure of what protocols to follow. I am not sure how to address them. I am not sure how I should be dressed. I am not sure of anything. Will you help me?'

Why was she asking him for help? Why did he seem like the kind of person whom everybody trusted? Why did he look like he knew all the answers? Gauri's mind wondered.

'Sure, why don't we take a walk outside in the forest for a while? Once you feel better, we can address your queries, one by one.'

They walked for what seemed like hours in complete silence. Gauri felt lighter with Shankar walking beside her. She was able to think more clearly and wasn't as tense as before. He made her feel like she could deal with her problems, one step at a time, and find her way back home. She noticed an aura around him, as if he was emanating positive energy—a cocoon of energy that was real and palpable.

Slowly, Gauri felt like she could be honest. 'Tell me about yourself,' she asked Shankar.

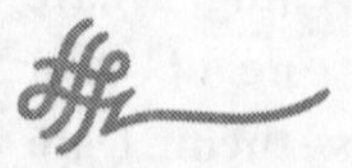

Shankar—a boy from nowhere

Maharaja Pashupati and Maharani Gautami were travelling back to Amara from Anagraha after the *ayushomam* of Chandrasekhara, their one-year-old baby. It was a traditional ritual that was performed in the maternal home of a new mother, invoking the blessings of the gods and praying for the long and healthy life of the newborn. The *pooja* was conducted with much pomp and fanfare, for Chandrasekhara was the heir to the throne of Saptapuri. The royal caravan was travelling back home through the Oundin mountain range and had camped for the night in a clearing in the dense jungles of the Soma Parvata.

At dawn, the royal priest travelling with them informed Pashupati that it was *pradosh*, an auspicious day for offering prayers to Lord Shiva. Pashupati, like all his forebears, had unwavering faith in the deity. His men gathered items for worship from the jungle and the king sat down with the queen in front of a makeshift clay *lingam* (in Shaivism, the lingam—often set within the yoni—serves as a profound symbol of Shiva's cosmic force, embodying the seamless cycle of creation, dissolution and rebirth through its abstract, pillar-like form) for the pooja. They were deeply immersed in their prayers when they heard a rustling sound.

To their surprise, just beyond their makeshift lingam, stood a young child, about three years old. He was dressed in sparse clothing like that of a mendicant, yet looked radiant and beautiful. The royal couple paused their prayers and began inquiring about the child. The ministers tried asking the child about his family, his home, etc. But the little boy was unable to provide any information. A search party was sent out to scout the nearby tribal settlements, villages or any signs of human inhabitation to locate the boy's family. Unfortunately, their efforts were in vain.

The boy could not be abandoned, so the royal priest agreed to take the child home. Upon reaching Amara, the queen personally took it upon herself to spread the word about the lost child. She had her artists paint portraits of the boy, which were circulated all over the kingdom with a message that if anyone who recognized the boy could collect him from the home of the royal priest.

Meanwhile, the priest took loving care of the boy. His daughter, Vidhushi, who was seven years old, was utterly pleased to have a companion to play with. She doted on the boy and took on all responsibilities for his care. Gautami regularly visited the child to see how he was doing. She kept up the search for his family for up to a year. Nobody ever came to claim the boy. It was as if he were a *swayambhu*, a self-manifested being. This was an apt description for a child who radiated a celestial and intangible glow and seemed unaware of his own origins.

It was only a matter of time before the priest and his daughter grew so fond of the boy that they welcomed him into their home forever. They named him Shankar. It was adorable to see how Vidhushi and Shankar got so friendly in such a short time.

From a young age, Shankar exhibited a maturity that was beyond his years. He often seemed lost in his thoughts and spoke little. But when he did, he was always polite and gentle. He was compassionate towards all living beings and deeply respected nature. He took great care of helpless creatures, young children and the elderly. He loved and respected Vidhushi deeply. She in turn played several roles in his life—that of a friend, sister and even a mother.

Vidhushi's mother had passed away due to an illness when she was only four years old, leaving a significant void in her life. This emptiness was filled by Shankar. He was the one person that brought her warmth, affection and pure joy.

Maharani Gautami was fond of Shankar right from the beginning. She ensured that he received an impeccable education. His rigorous weapons training was conducted alongside Prince Chandrasekhara. The two boys trained side by side, rain or shine, and over the years developed a strong bond. Maharaja Pashupati, too, began seeing Shankar for his abilities. He was a strong young man with patience, kindness and poise. He possessed courage and a fiery spirit. His leadership skills were exceptional and his decision-making was unmatched. He soon became a close confidante of the king.

Pashupati called on Shankar to help with several important decisions concerning the kingdom. These included organizing outdoor expeditions, training of the armed forces and conducting special missions for Amara, among others. It was Shankar who facilitated the marriage between Prince Chandrasekhara and Princess Indumathi of Sagara. He was the one who secured the marriage proposal from the kingdom of Sagara, situated on the eastern coast, for the crown prince.

One day, Shankar happened to meet Anandamayi. 'Meet' was a mild way to describe their first encounter. Shankar was asked by Pashupati to go to the outskirts of Amara where the secluded training centre for the Kabali, guardians of the Ajna Chakra, was located. Shankar was supposed to invite the head instructor of the Kabali, Acharya Jayapati, to a royal dinner being hosted for Chandrasekhara's birthday. As Shankar neared the centre, his horse suddenly tripped over some invisible barrier, and he flew off the horseback. He landed on his back when a sword came flying at him and landed within an inch of his right ear. Before he could get back on his feet, a strong leg landed on his neck, pinning him back to the ground. He looked up to see a feisty, hot-blooded woman staring down at him.

'How dare you trespass upon the training camp of the Kabalis?' she growled at him.

Shankar opened his mouth to explain, but she picked up her sword and pointed it at his face, grimacing at him.

'Think you can take advantage of our Acharya's absence?' It was then that Shankar noticed that his horse had been ambushed in a very clever way. The lady pinning him down had tied nearly invisible ropes between two trees and was lying in wait for anybody who dared set foot on these lands.

Shankar didn't get a chance to answer as Acharya Jayapati gasped. One look at the intruder and Jayapati almost passed out.

'Anandamayi, you brash woman. This is a trusted friend of mine and a confidante of the royal family,' he said. 'Let him up this instance.'

Shankar got up and dusted himself and thanked Jayapati. He went with the acharya to the training camp, while the woman, looking red-faced, followed them. Shankar presented the invitation to Jayapati and stayed a while to rest. In the evening, he thanked Jayapati for his hospitality and took his leave.

When he exited the perimeter of the training facility, he was accosted by the lady from his encounter during the day.

'Don't hurt me, my lady,' Shankar said, pretending to shiver in fear. He even brought his hands up and blocked his face from her view, as if to protect it.

She frowned. 'It's not funny. I apologize for my actions earlier today. I hope you will forgive me.'

'Consider it forgotten, my lady.'

She smiled for the first time that day and said, 'I am Anandamayi.'

'And I am Shankar,' he said. 'I salute your strength and courage. Few men are as brave as you are.'

From that day onwards, Shankar somehow became the only person whom Anandamayi confided in, spoke to or even cared about. He had won her trust even though he had done nothing out of the ordinary that day. She was a tough warrior who aspired to the post of warrior-in-chief of the Kabali. She never allowed herself a moment to make friends, socialize with people or even breathe, for that matter. Her sole purpose in life was to be an exceptional guardian of the sacred stone. Shankar was the only exception to this. He was her only friend. His sister was also someone whom Anandamayi engaged with in her free time. In the years to come, contrary to her views, and against her own will, Anandamayi would grow to love Shankar deeply in a romantic way.

Shankar went on to be appointed the *mukhya senapati*, the chief commander of the armed forces, of Saptapuri. He was the only person Pashupati had considered for the position following the retirement of his trusted commander-in-chief, Anghadwaj. Shankar became the eyes and ears of the king, fulfilling all his duties with utmost loyalty and consistently surpassing everyone's expectations.

Around the same time, Anandamayi was appointed as the

warrior-in-chief of the Kabali, becoming the youngest person ever to hold the position. She was also the first woman to be selected for the post since the contingent's inception, even though many women had been part of the Kabali over the past 700 years.

Meanwhile, Vidhushi had grown into an exceptional medical practitioner. She had studied under Guru Pratapeshwar, who had been the chief physician for the royal family for decades. After rigorous training, she went on to become his assistant, attending to the medical needs of the royals and the commoners. Eventually, she took over the position of Raj Vaidya when her guru decided to embrace *sannyasa*.

'It is very hard to emulate Shankar,' Vidhushi would tell Anandamayi with pride when they occasionally spoke. 'His disciplined life, his kindness, compassion, gallantry and moral fibre make him an outstanding human being. Sometimes, I wonder if he is from this world at all,' she added, with a twinkle in her eyes.

'What exaggeration,' said Anandamayi, rolling her eyes.

'Don't roll your eyes so far back, warrior woman. They'll get stuck there,' laughed Vidhushi.

Universal consciousness and inner-work

Shankar walked towards the royal chamber. 'Maharaja, the girl...' he began.

'Ah, yes. Gautami and I are going to visit her today.'

'There is no need for that, sir. She will join us for meals from now on. If you could speak to her then, she may feel less overwhelmed.'

'How do you do these things, Shankar? I heard that even Vidhushi could not manage to convince the girl, whatsoever.'

Shankar just smiled his familiar, magical smile. He couldn't tell why, but ever since he had rescued Gauri from the battle, he felt butterflies in his stomach every time he thought of her. This was unusual for him. Without realizing how he was reacting, his smile grew wider by the minute. He pulled himself together when Pashupati looked at him quizzically and waved his hands.

'We have a lot to discuss, Shankar. Gurupadaka's wounds have healed well, and he will be joining us for dinner this evening. We will have a full house today, and we need to address pressing issues. I am glad the girl will be joining us too. She might also get a feel of what we are all dealing with.'

Gauri entered the dining hall, feeling incredibly nervous. As she entered, she could feel every eye upon her, sizing her up, judging her and forming their opinions. She almost turned to leave when she spotted Shankar. He nodded at her reassuringly. Taking a deep breath, she moved towards him, and he stood up to greet her.

'I am pleased to introduce to Your Majesties, Gauri. Gauri, we have at the table…"

The multitude of names that followed was all a blur. It was very hard to remember them all. From what she gathered, there were at least two kings, one prince, a queen, ministers, royal teachers, chieftains and Vidhushi.

'We welcome you to our kingdom and hope that the rest of your stay with us is as uneventful and ordinary as you wish it to be, Gauri,' Gautami said politely. Pashupati and Chandrasekhara nodded in agreement.

'Please begin your dinner. You are free to leave when you are done, my dear. Our discussions and strategizing will continue well into the night,' said a concerned Pashupati.

Gauri thanked him and began eating her food.

'Welcome back from the dead, Guru, my friend,' said Shankar laughingly. 'I leave you alone for half a day on the battlefield, and you almost get yourself killed?'

'Yes, Shankar, we lost the battle only because you left,' quipped Gurupadaka in return.

'Finish your meals quickly and then let's get to work. This underground fort will not hold us for much longer. We need to work expeditiously,' Gautami said sharply.

Everyone ate faster, and one by one, they left the table and walked to an adjoining room. Vidhushi looked in Gauri's direction and told her that she was free to go to her room.

'I'd like to stay if that is not a problem,' Gauri said to everyone's surprise. 'Sure, why not,' replied Pashupati.

Animated discussion followed once everyone gathered in the adjacent room.

Pashupati: 'How are we going to hold our people here? We are incredibly low on supplies. This underground safe hold was not meant to house an entire kingdom. There is hardly any food left for the injured and fallen. Only the wounded and the sick should be staying here. The rest have to shift immediately.'

Gurupadaka: 'One party must go to the forest to open the hatch that connects us to the main fort. Pataleshwar and Adiparashakti are not directly connected, so that even if one location is compromised, the enemy would never find the other. All the women and children from our city have already been moved to the fortress and so have our food supplies. We only need to worry about the soldier now. It is a week-long journey once the hatch is opened, and we need to get this done soon.'

Pashupati: 'We need to regroup and go into battle one more time. We cannot stay in hiding forever. The Ajna Chakra is both our strength and our weakness. We cannot perish underground in trying to guard it.'

Chandrasekhara: 'Our spy, Chennu, returned this morning with the news that the demons are holding many prisoners in the two kingdoms that they had ravaged earlier. I suggest we free the prisoners. The able-bodied and strong amongst them can be recruited to fight for us.'

Shankar: 'I have sent envoys to kings Siddheshwara, Prajapati and Girijapati again. It is time they realized the significance of being on the right side. If an army of 30,000 soldiers had to go into hiding, their smaller armies do not stand a fighting chance against Moishan.'

Gautami: 'All three kings have come to their senses. We have received word that they need some time to gather their troops and join us. We have until the next waxing moon to prepare ourselves and gather enough soldiers, unless Moishan's army breaches our fort first.'

Pashupati: 'The Adiparashakti fortress will hold even under attack from 300 elephants. It is large enough to provide basic housing to our entire kingdom if needed. That is the only thing that we need not worry about today.'

Acharya Veni: 'Maharaja Pashupati, Raja Krishnakanth and members of this august gathering, you all need to address the elephant in the room. If we are unable to keep Moishan's army at bay for the second time, we will have no choice but to use the Ajna Chakra. Please be prepared for what may be inevitable.'

A deadly silence befell the room. This thought had weighed heavily upon Pashupati's mind ever since they had been forced into hiding. He had shared his fears with Gautami too.

Shankar: 'I hope, Acharya, that it will not come to that. We will be better prepared this time, for we have faced the demons once. We are more knowledgeable about their strengths, weapons, strategies and, most of all, their weaknesses. Prince Samara has returned to his kingdom to gather more troops. Even Princess Indumathi's brother's kingdom has offered what little they can do to help. Let us have faith that we will succeed this time.'

Chandrasekhara: 'Father, we need to form two groups of soldiers. One group should head to the ravaged kingdoms of Karnikapuri and Dwajasthapura to rescue the prisoners of war. All freed people should be sent to a new safe hold beyond Dwajasthapura. Only the strong and able should be brought back to the safety of our Adiparashakti fortress at Pravasi Lake. There will be wounded women and children among the prisoners, so the entire operation must be executed very carefully. Moishan's demons are sure to be on the lookout for us. They are currently rejoicing that we fled like mice from a sinking ship, but they won't let their guard down for long.

'As mother has pointed out, we have until the next waxing moon to prepare and gather our people. It gives us roughly a month before we can attack the Buffalo Demon and his army. We need to act quickly.'

Gurupadaka: 'Shankar and I will gather our strongest lieutenants and take the least conspicuous route to Karnikapuri.'

Chandrasekhara: 'My beloved minister, you are still recovering from surgery. It would not be wise for you to undertake a mission so dangerous. I can go with Shankar to Karnikapuri. Mother has agreed to go to the edge of the Soma Parvata and find the hatch to the tunnel that connects to the Pravasi Lake.

Pashupati: 'I will not allow the queen of this kingdom to put her life on the line. Let me do it.'

Gautami: 'The people need their king. If anything were to happen to you, who would lead them? The task of finding the hatch isn't that dangerous. I will take care of it.'

Krishnakanth: 'Then allow me the honour of going with you, my queen.'

Chandrasekhara: 'It is settled then. Mother and King Krishnakanth will travel to the edge of Soma Parvata. Shankar, we should prepare for our long and arduous journey. We will leave in three days, before dawn, under the cover of darkness.

The meeting was dismissed, and everyone left for their respective quarters. Gauri was among the first to leave. Her head was swimming with all the information she had received that evening. She felt like she was in a movie—the ones with the epic battles, sacrifices and noble heroes giving up their lives to save their people. She was exhausted by the time she reached her room. She fell asleep as soon as her head hit the pillow. Gauri had strange dreams that night—of elephants and horses and headless bodies on the ground—and she slept fitfully. She felt like she had barely off to sleep when a loud, rude knock at startled her awake. She groggily walked to the door and opened it.

'You were supposed to be at the clearing a while ago to begin your training,' Vidhushi said angrily.

'Wash up and go immediately,' she ordered. This woman either took her work as a healer very seriously or she was utterly protective of her brother and his time. Either way, Gauri wasn't in the mood to argue. She took a cold shower and, with quick, long strides, found her way to the forest floor.

There he was, looking as luminous as the morning sun, although the sun was still hours away from rising. He was dressed in a plain white cotton dhoti held in place by a cotton sash tied around his waist. The cloth that he usually wore across his upper body was missing, and he stood bare-chested in *vrikshasana* pose, his eyes closed. Gauri took a sharp breath and stopped in her tracks. She wondered if she should interrupt Shankar. Her breath alerted him, and he opened his eyes. He beckoned her to join him, and together they began their session.

They practised some basic kriyas and meditated for over two hours. Being a regular yoga practitioner who never missed her sessions back home, Gauri was able to cope easily with the different poses he taught. The only thing making her restless and distracted was the fact that she was not yet accustomed to draping a saree the way these people did. She also felt uncomfortable in the blouse, which left her shoulders and upper back bare. By the time they were done, so was her saree. It was loosely hanging on her, barely tucked in at one or two places. When she finished her meditation and stood up, her foot caught on a loose pleat in front of the saree, and the entire thing came undone.

Gauri gasped and tried to cover herself. Shankar at once closed his eyes and turned around. He walked away, mumbling something about fetching Vidhushi. In a flash, he disappeared among the trees. Gauri was left standing with the loose ends of her undone saree in her hand, wearing only a blouse and a petticoat. She moved behind a tree and peeped out. She could see Vidhushi approaching. Gauri went red with embarrassment. Strangely enough, Vidhushi seemed in a chirpy mood and was smiling about something.

'Gauri?' she called out. Gauri sheepishly stepped out from behind the tree. Vidhushi went ahead to swiftly undo and redo her saree. She smiled at Gauri in a very motherly fashion and said, 'Once you are done having your meal, I'll come down and teach you how to drape it properly. We can't have you accidentally tripping over your clothing and getting hurt again, can we?' She put her hand behind Gauri's back and guided her to her room.

That morning in the dining hall, people were busy going over their plans for the next few days. The kitchen staff was reviewing the food supplies available. Vidhushi's assistant, Karani was taking stock of the medical supplies. Both of these exercises were crucial for the upkeep and care of the wounded soldiers who were going to be left behind.

Gauri noticed that only Shankar was missing. 'Was it because of what had happened this morning?' she wondered. 'Shankar has gone down to the stables to check on the horses. The elephants have been left out in the forest with their mahouts, but the horses still need care here. Would you like to go see them?' asked Vidhushi, as if she had read her mind.

Gauri replied in the affirmative.

'Manikanta, could you please take Gauri down to the stables,' she asked one of the lieutenants standing near the door.

Manikanta looked honoured to lead Gauri to the stables. He didn't speak a word until he reached the horses. 'We are here, Devi,' he said and turned around and left.

Gauri entered the stable and looked around.

'These are beautiful and majestic beasts, aren't they?' said a familiar voice. Gauri spun around and came face to face with Shankar. He was standing so close to her that she could feel his breath. The corridor in the stables was very narrow, so she moved a little to the side to create a bit of distance between them.

'Would you like to ride one?' he asked.

'I don't know how to,' said Gauri.

He took her hand, saying, 'Come, I'll help you'.

Holding her close, he grasped her waist and hoisted her onto his horse. Suddenly, Gauri felt like her soul was singing. It was an unfamiliar yet warm sensation that she had never experienced before.

'This is Nandi, my best friend,' Shankar said, bringing her back to reality. This was the same horse he rode on the battlefield. She remembered its brown mane whipping her cheeks. Gauri patted his flank as Shankar hoisted himself up behind her. He held her hands and directed her on how to steer the horse. His large shoulders and arms completely enveloped her small frame as he tried to control his steed. Gauri felt free after a long time. She forgot her worries for a moment as the horse galloped through the forest, the canopied trees around them providing shade. Unfortunately, they couldn't venture too far from the underground fort, as it could attract the attention of the Moishan's spies.

Gauri felt secure around Shankar. Though he was a stranger, there was something about him that was very reassuring and heart-warming. She didn't worry, even if she wanted to, when he was around her. The two rode around for a long time and returned to the fort only when the sun was high above their heads.

Aside from her morning practice with Shankar, Gauri did not have much to do for the next two days. These early morning hours had become a time for disciplined and focused learning. As a teacher, Shankar was both intense and passionate. He sounded ecstatic, almost drunk, when he was teaching her about muscle strengthening, yoga, the body chakras and how to productively channelize inner energies.

'If physical and psychological strength are all that you're looking for, Gauri, you can easily attain that by rigorous exercising. But to make an inward journey of discovery, you must look beyond the physical. Activating just twenty-one chakras in your human system can vitalize the physical body.'

'But if you would like to transcend your limitations and become one with the cosmic greatness around you, then you must learn to light up all hundred and fourteen chakras in your system. If you can open your mind to new possibilities and be receptive, then you can truly find your higher self. I can teach you specific kriyas that will help your system adjust to your new surroundings, climate, food intake and changes in time zones. But if you want go beyond the mundane, I will teach you how to activate all your chakras. Your energies then can flow from the *mooladhara* chakra (situated at the base of the spine) towards the *sahasrara* chakra (situated at the top of the head),' he said intently.

Gauri seemed content to learn what her new guru was

teaching her. There had been no pressure on her from anybody in the fort to either accept the prophecy or become a valiant warrior. She wanted to focus on meditation because it gave her immense peace. In just two days, she felt a sense of quietude. She could sense her positivity returning and was able to think clearly without her mind being clouded by despair.

It helped her gain a new perspective on her situation. She saw the goodness of the king, his leaders and his subjects. They all deserved a fair chance to protect their treasure and their people. She said a silent prayer to her gods for Saptapuri's victory.

That evening, at the dinner table, Gauri surprised even herself by asking the Maharaja, 'Your majesty, I would like to accompany the troops going to Karnikapuri with your permission.'

The entire table looked aghast. No one had expected this complete change of heart. Some were secretly relieved because they thought she had finally come to her senses and would take her rightful place in the war. Others thought that she would be an unnecessary burden since she was not a warrior. Prophecy or not, most people by now had begun to think that Gauri's arrival was simply a random accident.

Krishnakanth said, 'This is a perilous mission, my child. You better stay back here, where you'll be watched over by our people.'

'She will be going with exceptional warriors like Chandrasekhara and Shankar. What is there to worry? She is doing nothing at the fort, anyway. I say, let her go,' said Maharani Gautami.

Vidhushi seconded the maharani's opinion. 'Maybe stepping out into the world and exploring it may give her the tools she needs to find her way back to her land. She will find nothing to help her down here.'

It was agreed that Gauri would leave with the troops headed for Karnikapuri early next morning. Manikanta was sent to help her gather and pack her things. He was a helpful lad and was very talkative this time around. He was extremely curious about her life back home and incessantly questioned her about what was it like, what she did there and how she ended up on the battlefield. Some of her responses amazed him; some he was sceptical about and at some he laughed outright. Gauri had not felt this light-hearted in a long time. Manikanta reminded her of her childhood friend Bhadrachalam. After they were done with the packing, Manikanta wished her good night and carried her bags off to the caravan.

Dawn came, and with it, the silent, cat-like movement of the troops. Led by Chandrasekhara and Shankar, the group consisted of fifty soldiers. Everyone was atop their horse and moving quietly in a line, one behind the other. It was a three-day-long journey to Karnikapuri, and they had to be incredibly careful not to attract the attention of the enemy soldiers. During the day, when they camped, the cooking was done in a deep, cauldron-like drum. Made of copper and lined on the inside with baked clay, this special apparatus had two levels: a lower level with a door and an upper covered compartment. The fire was lit at the bottom of the drum, and the door was closed. Food was then placed on the upper level, and the top was sealed off. The food was cooked using indirect heat, resulting in little smoke. Any small amount that did escape was immediately dissipated into the air with a fan fashioned from leaves. This ensured that no smoke rose into the sky, as that would have compromised their position, even in such a dense jungle as this.

Even during their journey, Shankar ensured that Gauri continued with her yoga. He expected her to wake up well before the rest of the group and meditate and exercise. 'If you cannot be single-minded and focused on your *sadhana* (practice), you will never be able go beyond the mundane.'

The journey was difficult for Gauri, as she was not accustomed to spending long hours on horseback. Her body ached in unusual places; muscles that she didn't even know existed were sore and bothering her. Her single-minded focus on her meditation and yoga was the only reason she was able to make it through each day. That, and Manikanta's company. The young lieutenant was expressive, talkative and curious; he could chatter all day. He rode his horse alongside Gauri's and kept her engaged. The other members of the troop always kept their distance from her. She didn't know if it was out of reverence or because they couldn't be bothered with a woman who wasn't anywhere in their league.

'You are cluttering your mind with unnecessary thoughts. Clutter will weigh down your journey, gentle one,' Shankar said softly. Gauri was startled. It was as if Shankar had read her mind. How could he know what she was thinking about?

He had trotted up to her left, looked at her face, drinking in its features, and wished he could absorb all her anxieties. Her face was creased with worry, evident from her furrowed eyebrows. Her brows arched over her doe-like brown eyes, which shone softly. Her pink, small lips were quizzically twisted towards one side.

'Focus on what your heart wants. Do not waver. What others think of you should not bother you. Their perception is influenced by their limited mindset. You are what you choose to be, Gauri.' Gauri smiled at Shankar, and he moved his horse further along.

To arrive at their destination, they had to climb a steep slope and then descend sharply. The horses couldn't make the steep climb with their riders, so the last leg of the journey was done on foot, each man leading his horse up the mountainside. The forest of Jhoomar was filled with summer blossoms, and the forest floor was covered in leaves and flowers of distinct colours.

It was just past lunch on the third day of the journey, and the men were resting. One of them was leaning against the trunk of a large teak tree and humming a tune. Suddenly, he shrieked as if he were being attacked. Irritated, people turned to look, only to see a long black snake slithering away. The venom was spreading rapidly, and the man was writhing in agony. Chandrasekhara cleaned the man's wound at once and made him lie comfortably. Another soldier bandaged the bite loosely. But the man looked pale and extremely sick.

'One of us will have to stay back with him as he cannot travel any further now. If the snake is venomous, there is little that we can do. But if it isn't, we can apply some herbs on his wound and let him rest. Let me have a look around the place,' Shankar said.

Shankar left to look for the herbs. Being around Vidhushi had taught him a thing or two about medicine. The rest of the members waited in silence. Suddenly, an arrow whizzed out of nowhere and hit the tree just inches above where the injured soldier lay. Everyone scrambled for their weapons and tried to find cover. The injured soldier was pulled behind a large tree with some help. Within moments, the area was surrounded by ten large, fair, troll-like people.

Chandrasekhara mouthed some silent orders to his soldiers. Slowly, they began to pan out, remaining hidden behind trees and bushes. The largest of the demon soldiers shouted something in a tongue they didn't understand. To Chandrasekhara's horror, the enemy stepped into the open and held Shankar at the point of a large, jagged blade. He looked triumphant and talked continuously. Shankar was slightly wounded; there was blood at the corner of his lips and his face looked a little swollen.

Out of nowhere, an arrow whooshed past Shankar's face and hit the ogre square in the forehead. He fell, releasing Shankar as he did. This was the opening they had all been looking for, and the soldiers jumped out and attacked the demon soldiers. A struggle ensued between the two sides, ending in Moishan's men being decimated. It was a blood bath, and the forest floor had changed colour.

Gauri finally came out of hiding to find Chandrasekhara hugging Manikanta tightly. 'Your quick thinking has saved my best friend and our best warrior. I cannot thank you enough.'

'I was only performing my duty, my prince,' he replied, completely embarrassed by the attention bestowed upon him.

Shankar called their attention to a pressing issue. 'We were either accidentally discovered by this small band of barbarians, or the enemy has wised up to our movements. I think it is the former. In any case, we need to get out of here as fast as possible. We cannot leave behind any man as we had planned before. We shall carry the wounded on horseback. I have the herb here.' He crushed the leaves in his hand and smeared the paste on the man's wound.

Gauri had just fully understood the magnitude of the deep trouble that Saptapuri was facing. The soldiers that had attacked them did not even look human. Her mind travelled back to the tales her grandfather told her, especially the one about the demon king of Lanka who had kidnapped Lord Rama's wife. She now felt a renewed awe for Indian epics.

The men finally reached the outer edge of the forest that bordered Karnikapuri. It was decided that they would break up into groups of seven to eight men and leave their horses and possessions hidden in the jungle. The wounded soldier had survived the night, and it looked like he would live. He was left behind with the soldier who had helped bandage him.

'Stay well hidden, my men. May Mahadev be with you,' Shankar said. Just before leaving the camp, Shankar gave Gauri a sword, helping her fasten the sword belt around her waist.

'What would I do with this? I do not even know how to use it,' she said. 'Just in case, my lady,' Shankar replied.

From this point forward, they were to proceed to the town on foot, spreading out in three different directions. Later, they were to regroup and discuss a course of action based on the findings of each group. Gauri was accompanied by Manikanta, Shankar and four other soldiers.

The cruel king from a strange land

He roared and banged the head of the messenger into the thick, engraved arms of his throne. At the end of each arm was the sculpted head of a fierce-looking buffalo with gigantic, thick horns. With a bleeding forehead, the messenger looked up at his master for further instructions. What he received, instead, was a kick to his chest that sent him flying several feet backwards. The messenger dared not stand up; he lay on the floor, whimpering.

'How?' he bellowed, flecks of spit flying from his mouth. His face was livid with anger. His nostrils flared and his thick, bushy brows came so close together that they were almost fused into one. He leaned forward menacingly and lifted his elephantine foot, as if he wanted to stamp the very life out of the person that had dared to deliver the news that he had been bested.

Who could do this to HIM—the conqueror of worlds, the omen of terror, the harbinger of death and destruction?

His bloodlust had to be satiated somehow. He wanted to kill the messenger and hang him up outside his tent. Moishan's rage was unchecked. His brothers, Shumran and Nishan, rushed to pull the messenger off the floor and hurried him out of the chamber.

'How?' he repeated, even though he was all alone now.

Moishan roared to his deputies, 'Find them, you imbeciles. Or I will gut every last one of you. Use your brains, brawn, stealth or cunning. I don't care. Do not return without information and the heads of some enemy soldiers.'

Seven nights had come and gone since the cowards of Saptapuri had run away from the battlefield and hidden themselves. Moishan had his men hunt for them day night, but in vain. The kingdom lay deserted; they had abandoned everything and gone into hiding. Such a thing had never happened to him before. The rats had planned their escape well, he thought.

They had taken with them the very thing that he was desperately seeking. The fabled Ajna Chakra. What fools would hold such power yet never use it? They didn't deserve to have it. He did! The bravest warrior in the world, one who dared to dream beyond boundaries, territories and kingdoms. He could conquer the world. He would be master of all lands.

He had come a long way from his humble beginnings by taking what he liked—snatching it from the hands of others, never asking and never by playing nice. Now, if he could get his hands on the sacred stone, he would become immortal, undefeated and unchallenged forever! Although he was getting restless, he thought to himself, 'how long could they hide?' Eventually, they would run out of food and water. Moishan had waited for years to come this far. He can wait a few more days.

He thought back to his humble beginnings…

It was a terribly cold year. The people of the northern province of Kitan were being pressured by the ruthless leader of the neighbouring state to bow down to his rule or die of cold and misery. The leader of the Kitan province was a spineless individual. Although his army was larger than that of the neighbouring state, he lacked the qualities to unite his people and fight back. Shirak allowed his people to rot, always wringing his hands helplessly.

Things had reached a point where it became virtually impossible to ward off hunger and cold any longer. Every single day, one of Shirak's close aides approached him to do something. He pleaded at the feet of the leader, but in vain. From the sidelines, the aide's youngest son watched the constant imploring and begging. He was a well-built child for an eleven-year-old, larger than his siblings, even though he was the youngest of the six. He beat his brothers and took their food simply because he could and because he wanted to. He was ruthless.

A day came when he could no longer stand his father grovelling at the feet of Shirak. He picked up a club that his father had set down and bludgeoned him to death, all the while screaming, 'You are so weak and pathetic!'

Covered in blood, he looked at Shirak and said, 'Are you ready to fight now?' Stunned, Shirak meekly agreed.

The boy marshalled his people and attacked the neighbouring province. They hacked to death every man who stood and ravaged the towns. The boy felt exhilarated by all the violence and bloodletting. He wanted more. He gathered more troops and attacked all the nearby provinces without an iota of mercy. Soon, his name began to be feared.

People were terrified of him and his conquests. Words of Moishan's evil deeds began to travel farther than his conquests.

When Moishan was in his late twenties, he heard tales of a kingdom far south of his homeland. He had heard that they had a stone that could make one immortal. He began to crave the stone. He wanted more power. He wanted to rule the whole earth, forever.

So, he began his journey towards the southern lands. He left the snowy mountains behind and came down to lands where the snow melted and flowed as rivers. His cruelty and ruthlessness knew no bounds. He conquered. He fought. He despoiled kingdom after kingdom.

In one of the battles, a prince dared to attack him. He stabbed Moishan and then took a large club-like weapon and landed a heavy blow, almost splitting his head open. Moishan fought back and ripped out the heart of the prince, before losing consciousness.

The wounds from that battle physically disfigured him forever. The blow to his head had resulted in the growth of two tumours that protruded just above his forehead, almost like horns. This had earned him the nickname of 'Buffalo Demon'. He enjoyed the name and revelled in the fear that it elicited.

As he travelled further south in his quest for the fabled stone, he learned that the land he searched for was protected by an enormous and formidable mountain range called Oundin. He laughed cynically; these mortal fools didn't know where he came from. His homeland was up in the cold, snow-clad mountains. He had crossed many unforgiving and treacherous terrains as part of his quest. After spending twelve long years searching for this stone, he wasn't going to give up because of a mere mountain range. He would annihilate them all, raze everything in his path to the ground. He would conquer until there was nothing left to conquer.

Walking through a ghost town

They entered what had once been a bustling town, now reduced to dust. Gauri looked around her in despair. The foul creatures of Moishan's army had plundered and pillaged everything. Not a pillar stood in its rightful place. They had massacred the men, raped the young girls and widows alike and had not even spared the children. Gauri stepped on what looked like the femur bone of a young child. She wanted to vomit. Her eyes burned with tears, and her insides knotted so tightly that she experienced real, physical pain. The town was nothing but a ghost town. Nothing stirred. Everything stood still. Even the rats and rodents had abandoned the place.

What monster was capable of such merciless atrocities? It was horrific. As Gauri looked around, her blood boiled, and she seethed in anger. Lost in thought, she grasped the hilt of the sword so tightly that its edge dug into her palm, drawing blood.

'Your blood is too precious, Devi. Save it for a more important occasion,' said Manikanta, loosening her grip on the blade.

Gauri was sobbing by now.

'Who I am or where I come from doesn't matter anymore.

I may never find my way back home. But if I stay here and just watch these barbarians destroy everything you hold sacred and precious, I may never sleep in peace again. I may not be a warrior, but I am going to do my best to be of help. I want to see this through to the end, whatever it may be.'

Manikanta dropped to his knees and, sobbing like a child, he touched Gauri's feet. Gauri stepped back, embarrassed.

Watching this, Shankar, who was standing behind them smiled. The student was ready. He remembered Vidhushi's words, 'Acceptance is the first step.'

They didn't need to split into three groups as they had quickly located the prisoners of war. The captives were locked up in large cages, had not been fed for days and appeared to be on the verge of death. There were many young boys amongst the prisoners. Why had Moishan kept so many of them alive was a question that plagued their mind.

It also became clear that the men who guarded these prisoners were the ones who had attacked Shankar and now lay dead in the forest of Jhoomar. The soldiers freed the prisoners first. Among them, there was one man who was well past his prime, and his body was old and shrivelled. He told the men from Saptapuri that he had been spared because he understood the enemy's language, having spent many years travelling as a merchant. Moishan's men had told him that he might be of use to them later if negotiations were needed with the 'cowardly kings'. Although they also told him that the possibility of that was extremely remote, as the Buffalo Demon only believed in conquests and not negotiations.

He further recounted the horrific atrocities inflicted by the Buffalo army. He explained that the young boys were kept alive to be trained as merciless soldiers. The women were spared, only to be enjoyed as fruit of labour by the disgusting soldiers of the buffalo army.

Shankar and the group shuddered upon hearing this. It became clear that they couldn't, at any cost, let this beast defeat them. It felt as if humanity itself was at stake because of one man. Shankar ordered his men to begin scouting the countryside for food to feed the prisoners. They couldn't possibly journey onward with such weak men, women and children. Twenty soldiers along with Chandrasekhara stayed behind to take care of the prisoners. Shankar and the rest went in search of food. It would have to be a quick search. They had lots to do. The freed prisoners had to be separated by age, gender, and capabilities. The able-bodied had to travel with the Saptapuri soldiers towards Dwajasthapura. The prisoners of war had to be freed there as well. The weak, the women, and the children had to be safely hidden away safely in the surrounding areas.

While searching for food in the ruins and the adjoining plantations and orchards, Gauri spotted a derelict alchemist's shop. She couldn't hold her excitement when she found several chemicals that were in a usable condition. She went berserk thinking of the possibility of recreating the liquid mix that had exploded and transported her to this ancient land. Gauri pocketed as many chemical compounds as she possibly could, without anyone noticing, before moving on.

Finding enough food became a problem. The Buffalo army had burnt everything that could be planted, grown or harvested. They had also killed cattle and taken the meat to feed themselves. With a lot of effort, Shankar and his men managed to find enough to feed the prisoners for two nights. Now, they needed to figure out a way to keep them safe and out of sight.

'We don't know how long the war is going to drag on. How

can we keep these many people hidden without food or means for survival? The question came from one of the soldiers who had accompanied Chandrasekhara and Shankar.

'We will have to come up with something soon,' replied Shankar.

The solution came from the old prisoner whom they had freed. 'Son, three miles from here, flows the beautiful river Tapasi. There are mountains bordering one side of the riverbank. I have heard that there are crevices in the mountains that lead to huge underground caves. We should gather as much food as possible and find these caves to hide in. That way, we can be out of sight for up to two full moons from now.'

'But what if we do not defeat Moishan's army by then, sir?' asked Chandrasekhara.

'Even if we run out of food and perish from hunger, we can die in peace and that is surely better than to die at the hand of these monsters.'

'We will free the prisoners of Dwajasthapura too and lead them to the same caves, if possible,' said Shankar, 'assuming we find the caves before we ourselves are discovered.'

The group from Saptapuri decided that they should split up. Gauri was to stay with Manikanta and fifteen more soldiers. They were tasked with finding as much food as possible with the help of the able-bodied men from Karnikapuri. Gauri and Manikanta were specifically given the task of finding the underground caves.

Shankar, Chandrasekhara, and the rest of the men left the next morning for Dwajasthapura. They were concerned that the Buffalo army had likely gotten wind of their movements by now, making it tougher to free the prisoners from the next kingdom. Nonetheless, they went ahead.

The hidden caves

Gauri and Manikanta guided the tired and wounded people as they walked along the edge of the forest for two days under the scorching sun. Fortunately, the soldiers managed to shoot two deer in the jungle. One deer was cooked and fed the crowd well for the next three days, while the other was only partially cooked and carried along for later use. On the third day, they finally reached the riverbank. The people were exhausted, but they were exhilarated to see fresh water and fruit trees lining the riverbank.

Gauri and Manikanta scoured and ferreted around in the hot sun, searching for a cave mouth or a crevice that extended more than half a mile. They found one when dusk had almost taken over. It was a deep, narrow gap between two rock faces. Unsure of whether it led anywhere, Manikanta tied a thick rope around his waist and lowered himself down the gap. The descent was steep—almost a mile deep—and just when he thought he was getting nowhere, his feet touched the soft, cool sand. He hoisted himself back to the top with the help of Gauri. They decided to wait until dawn to do a thorough check before leading people to the cave.

When Manikanta and Gauri returned to the riverbank, they sensed that something was wrong. There was a visible blood trail, and they feared the worst. They were surprised to find that the people, along with a few Saptapuri soldiers, had overpowered two Buffalo army soldiers. They were bound to the trees, almost lifeless, but not dead. Gauri was quick to think.

She said, 'If we kill them and leave their bodies, we will alert the enemy to our presence here, which could lead them straight to us. I suggest that we tie them to logs and let them float down the river. The currents and rapids will take them far away from here. It will be a while before they can pass on a message to anyone, assuming they survive the river.'

'Also, we should take the risk and move to the underground caves right away, before we lose sunlight. Staying out here for another night in the open would only invite more trouble,' added Manikanta.

After they all agreed on a plan, the soldiers carefully led each person, one by one, down the crevice. Gauri was the first to descend and used a makeshift torch to light a fire. As more people came down, several torches were lit, allowing them to explore their surroundings. It was a beautiful and extensive underground network of tunnels with soft sand as the base. At some point, the river water had formed a small rivulet below, running for four miles before disappearing into the face of the mountain. It likely emerged on the other side as a picturesque waterfall. The presence of the rivulet was ideal as it provided both fresh water and fish for food.

Manikanta and two other soldiers took turns to watch the mouth of the crevice from a hideout in the mountains. Perched at a vantage point, they would have been able to spot Shankar and the crew when they eventually made their way here, along with any enemy movement.

Very few people in Dwajasthapura had survived Moishan's incursion. Two soldiers from the Buffalo army were guarding hundred and fifty prisoners of war. The troops easily overcame the two guards but had to kill them because they put up fierce resistance.

Surprisingly, Moishan's army had not destroyed all supplies in Dwajasthapura like they did in Karnikapuri. There were plenty of grains left in stores, intact and edible. Prince Chandrasekhara, Shankar and their men, along with the freed prisoners and all the rations that they could carry, headed back to Kamala, the capital of Karnikapuri. They travelled for four days before reaching the banks of the river Tapasi, where mountains bordered it on one side.

Manikanta was relieved to see his future king and the rest of the men. He led them to the hideout, where everyone could rest a while and refresh themselves. The people of Karnikapuri were overjoyed to see the grains that had been reclaimed from Dwajasthapura. It meant that they will have enough food while they were in hiding.

The prince and his men were now ready to return to their fortress near Lake Pravasi. Their quest to save the prisoners of the two fallen kingdoms was successful. They had mustered the support of five hundred able-bodied men who had joined their force after being freed. They began their journey back to Pataleshwar.

The journey would have been shorter if they travelled by the Tapasi river, which at some point merged with the Narmada river, leading them to the mouth of the Lake Pravasi. But this meant risking being out in the open waters for two days. Also, they didn't have a ship large enough to carry five hundred men. The only choice was to cut right through the

Jhoomar forest and then cross over into Bhanre forest.

Chandrasekhara was fervently hoping that his mother had found the opening to the tunnel that was the only covert way to go from the underground fort to the fortress by Lake Pravasi.

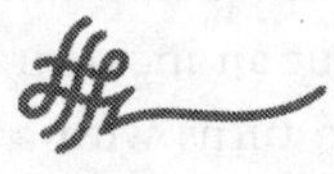

A general like none other

Moishan and his warriors had camped just outside the capital city of Amara. They had not destroyed the city yet. Since all its inhabitants were in hiding, they could take whatever supplies they wanted. The Buffalo Demon intended to lay siege to the city until the people of Saptapuri reached the point of starvation and crawled out of their rat holes to die at his hands. He would then take pleasure in killing every one of them. He would carve the flesh off the king's back while he was still alive, forcing him to endure excruciating pain, just as the king had inflicted on Moishan by keeping him away from the sacred stone. He shuddered in excitement, imagining the Ajna chakra in his hand. He had finally learned the name of the object he was after. It was not a legend; it was real, it was palpable. He was so close to it now that he could feel the hair on his arms standing on end. It was an intoxicating feeling.

Moishan and his brothers were drinking some intoxicant that they found in the palace brewery. It tasted excellent. The brothers, Shumran and Nishan, were much older than Moishan. But they had learned the hard way to take orders from him and listen to him, lest their heads be bludgeoned like their father's had been. The brothers were amusing each other with stories about the soldiers and their escapades with women. They had defiled every woman who had survived their spree of mass destruction. Nishan spoke in a sleazy manner about an incident in the town of Kamala, where the men had taken turns with a particularly beautiful woman until she stabbed herself to death to release herself from their clutches.

All this made Moishan lustful. In a complete state of intoxication, he called upon Raakat, his most loyal general, and said, 'Bring me the most beautiful woman amongst all the prisoners. Tell her that the conqueror of the world wants her.'

Raakat knew that the city of Amara was a ghost town and that he would have to journey back to Kamala or Dwajasthapura to bring women. However, he did not dare incur the wrath of Moishan. So, he bowed low to pay his respects, and left.

'Saddle up the horses,' Raakat barked at one of the lowest-ranking soldiers. 'We are going hunting for the supreme master.' He spat on the ground in irritation and disgust.

The sarcasm in his voice and his actions was unmistakable. He had grown tired of the constant travel. There was never a time when they spent more than a few months in one place. It was conquest after conquest. Raakat sometimes dreamed of simply settling down—having a woman, raising a family, eating and sleeping in peace. For twelve years, he had followed Moishan faithfully as they conquered all the lands south of the cold, stony Cho Oyu mountains. The yellow-skinned men had known no other way of life. They took pleasure in splitting people's heads into two or swinging an axe to gut a man or drive a sword through someone's heart. They took pride in destroying villages, vandalizing homes, plundering and looting cities. They revelled in molesting and despoiling women.

He hadn't given much thought to any of this until recently. He had been content following orders, looting, pillaging and marauding. However, lately, he had grown tired of this life. It began with the thought what would happen once Moishan got the stone. What would come next? More pillaging, more plundering and more destruction to satisfy his insatiable lust for power. They would keep fighting and moving from one place to another. There would never come a time when they could simply retire and enjoy what they had earned so far.

There were days when Raakat would just wish that he would be killed in the next battle. Then it would all be over. He would finally be delivered from his tiresome life. But until then, he was bound to serve Moishan, lest he suffer a shameful death, bereft of all honour, at the hands of the demon lord. For now, he had to hunt for the savage's next prey.

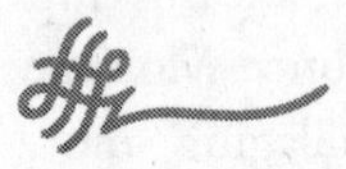

The trapdoor in the forest

Maharani Gautami and Raja Krishnakanth had left the Pataleshwar fort to find the hatch and open the tunnel doors leading to Adiparashakti fort by Lake Pravasi. The two scouted the jungles of Bhanre for three days but found nothing. Their frustration was growing as the Maharani worried about the welfare and safety of her people. 'How well is this hatch door hidden,' exclaimed Krishnakanth, in frustration, on the afternoon of the third day.

Gautami burst into laughter.

'Is this funny?' he asked her.

'Certainly,' she answered. 'Do you not see the irony of your question? The door was designed to be hidden well to protect the tunnel, and thereby safeguard our people in times of need. What good would it be if everyone who passed by could figure out that there was a hidden door that provided access to secret tunnels.'

Krishnakanth smiled. 'You are right, your Majesty. I suppose it is the heat and fatigue that is making me frustrated. I hope our search is not utterly futile.'

'Why don't we rest for a while, Raja Krishnakanth? Frustration only saps your energy and hinders your ability to complete the task at hand,' replied Gautami. 'I see some boulders against the hillocks behind us. We can rest our backs against these. The trees on the side will provide the much-needed break from the sun too.'

He nodded in agreement and the two walked towards the boulders. They sat down to rest and Gautami took out some food that they had packed for the journey. She handed some to Krishnakanth and began eating some herself.

'May I ask you a question?' Krishnakanth said hesitantly.

'Sure,' said Gautami. 'I think you want to know why I chose Pashupati at the swayamvara all those years back?'

Krishnakanth looked baffled by how she had read his mind. "But…How…Yes,' he mumbled.

'Both of your skills were at par. You had both completed the first task successfully and brought the two Neelkants to my father. He then sent the birds to my chamber to adorn the golden cages that had been built for them. When I went up to my chamber that night, I saw the birds looking forlorn. I couldn't understand why anyone would want to cage such beautiful creatures. My father didn't realize that I preferred seeing these birds chirping in the gardens and soaring high above in the sky, savouring a kind of freedom that we can only dream of, and not trapped in cages. How did it matter to the birds that the cage was made of gold? To them, it was just a prison. I went to the cages, watched them closely for a while and talked to them before setting them free. It was then that I noticed that one of the birds had been roughed up. Its feathers were bent out of shape, and it looked afraid. I enquired with the handmaid who had brought them to my room and learnt that the distressed bird was the one that you had caught.'

'I released both birds, but your bird couldn't fly. It was hurt. I left the cage open and nursed it back to health over the next few days until she voluntarily flew away. But that night, I had made up my mind that Pashupati was the man that I wanted to marry. He seemed to have a gentle side, which was important for me. I wasn't just looking for a strong, spirited king. I also wanted a caring, compassionate husband. In my mind, one had to be both a good king as well as a good human being. I prayed to the lord for Pashupati to win the contest the next day. I was relieved when father left the choice to me, and I was able to select him.'

Krishnakanth smiled and then asked, 'Has he lived up to it?'

'Yes, he has. He wouldn't even hurt an ant. I know how much pain this battle has caused him. He is a good king who has taken lives to save lives in this battle. But I know that this has caused him immeasurable angst.'

'I pray to Shiva and Shakti to bestow upon us a miracle that may deliver us from this abhorrent situation,' said a humbled Krishnakanth.

'When did you decide to let go of the perceived humiliation of that day?' Gautami asked Krishnakanth curiously.

'When I met my wife. Tara was the most beautiful, sweet and kind person that I had met. She was the daughter of my father's friend who ruled the neighbouring kingdom. She has made me a better person. She saw beyond my brash personality and found an equable man beneath it. The day she accepted my proposal, all my hate and anger vanished for good.'

It was Gautami's turn to smile. 'She is a lucky queen,' she added.

'Oh Shankara!' exclaimed Krishnakanth, suddenly.

'What?' asked Gautami, jumping to her feet and grabbing her sword. She furtively looked around as if expecting someone to jump out from behind the trees.

'No, no, calm down,' said Krishnakanth. 'I just realized that these boulders do not appear to be a natural extension of the hillocks. Look at their formation. The circular set up seems unnatural. I believe that we may have to do some digging now.'

Gautami went to the horse and brought back two large shovels. She looked at him questioningly.

He picked up the equipment and began digging, while Gautami started digging a few feet away from him. After what seemed like a fair amount of time, Krishnakanth had dug a hole that was seven or eight feet deep.

Gautami was beginning to think this exercise was an exercise in futility when his tool hit something hard with a metallic clank. They both smiled. Gautami moved closer to Krishnakanth, and they began digging with renewed energy until they had freed the door. It took a humungous effort and a lot of tugging and heaving on their part, but they managed to prise the door open. It opened onto a flight of stairs spiralling downwards into a dark space. The stairway was narrow and circular, allowing one person at a time to come through. It was damp and covered in moss. The stones that made up the stairway were cut unevenly, some small and some large. The height between each step varied as well.

'Be careful! These steps are a nasty piece of work and slippery too,' called out Krishnakanth, who went down the stairs first. His voice echoed in the narrow, deserted stairwell.

Krishnakanth had reached the bottom of the stairway. 'You better stop on the last step, Maharani,' he said. 'There isn't enough space for the two of us to stand together.'

Gautami joined him a moment later, stopping at the last step. The narrow stairwell ended in a small alcove with high walls of stone to their left and right and facing them. The wall in front of them had a small iron door. It was only three and a half feet in height and was shaped like an arch. To the right of the stairwell was another door like the one they faced. Both doors had been designed in such a way that one would have to get down on all fours and crawl to get through. It took a lot of energy to unlatch these doors. It was surprising that years of neglect had not led these iron doors to rust even though the stairwell seemed damp.

Krishnakanth bent down and crawled into the tunnel behind the first door. This gave Gautami space to inspect the other door. Behind each door was a long winding tunnel that led away from the staircase. Which tunnel led where was hard to say, but based on their sense of direction, both agreed that the tunnel facing the stairs led to Pataleshwar, the underground fort, and the tunnel to the right led to Adiparashakti, the lakeside fortress. Having inspected it for safety, the two concluded that the tunnels didn't pose any danger to troops who would use them to move from one location to another. They left both doors open and climbed back up the stairs to the surface.

'We must close the trapdoor from above and bury it under the sands again. Nobody should ever get wind of the door's existence,' said Gautami.

After exiting the staircase, they closed the hatch door shut. They bolted it back the way they found it and swiftly buried it with all the sand they had dug up. They got onto their horses and rode over the place several times until the entire area was covered in hoofprints. It left no signs that someone had recently dug the place up.

The two then found their way back to the underground fortress with the good news and were greeted with much joy. All the members of the allied forces began preparing for moving through the tunnels to the Adiparashakti fortress.

Vidhushi refused to leave her patients behind. She said, 'I will help them recover. They need my care. You will probably be going into battle after forty nights. I will join you then. If there is any change in the plan, send a message and I will join you. For now, let me do my duty as a physician.'

The Adiparashakti fortress

The soldiers began their journey from one fort to another. They were happy, for they would be able to see their family, children and parents once they reached the Adiparashakti fortress. When they reached the alcove, each man bent down and crawled into the stairwell and crawled out through the other door into the next tunnel. Their possessions were pushed to them by the men behind and taken through by the men ahead. Each man helped the other to make it through to the connecting tunnel. It took them a week to finally get to the main fort by the lakeside.

Anandamayi was relieved as she received the king, the queen and several members of the allied forces into the main fort. The Ajna Chakra and the Kabali guarding it had been discreetly moved into the fort on the second day of the first battle, along with almost all the women, children and elderly people of Amara. Although Anandamayi understood the importance of protecting the stone with her troops, she felt bitter about being left out of the battle. She had spent the last eight days having nightmares about the battle. She was tormented by thoughts about who had survived, who had fallen and who was injured? She wished that she could be out there helping them.

When the troops arrived, Anandamayi sighed with relief. She was ecstatic to see Pashupati, Gautami, Acharya Veni,

Gurupadaka and Krishnakanth. But her face fell and her soul was crushed when she realized that three key members had not returned. Where were Chandrasekhara, Shankar and Vidhushi?

Princess Indumathi had the same query. Her child Tanmay was missing his father, and she too was yearning to see the safe return of Prince Chandrasekhara.

Anandamayi looked enquiringly towards Gurupadaka. He said, 'Let us fill you in at mealtime. Please make arrangements for all the people who have arrived to be fed and taken to their resting quarters first.'

Anandamayi nodded and went off to make the necessary arrangements. Though it was a happy time, it was tinged with sadness too. It was quite a sight watching children greet their fathers and wives thanking the gods that their husbands had returned. Parents were also celebrating the return of their sons.

It was also a time for grief. There were many a woman who had waited for their men to return but were crushed, knowing they would never come back. Many others were told that their men were gravely injured and were being treated by Vidhushi at the Pataleshwar fort. These women were now very keen to be by the side of their loved ones. It was heartbreakingly difficult to explain to them that resources were limited and that it would not be possible to make multiple trips between the two safe holds.

'Your brave husbands are in the hands of the best medical practitioner in the land. Vidhushi refused to come back with us to care for the injured and wounded. Their bravery will have been in vain if you spend the meagre resources we have on travelling up and down between the two places. How will we feed our children if we run out of supplies just to accommodate the transportation of a few people back and forth?' pleaded Gurupadaka.

'You are fortunate that you have news of your loved ones, even though you are separated from them. Think for a moment of all the soldiers who fought with us and have families in other kingdoms. There is no way to convey the news about their well-being or the loss of their men to their families,' said Gautami pleadingly.

A mighty general

A few miles away in the city of Amara, Moishan was getting restless. Not only had he never waited this long to conquer a kingdom, but he had also never stayed in a ghost town. This meant that his secondary source of entertainment, women, was absent here. He loved the smell of their skin, the way they screamed and the sound of their delicate bones getting crushed under his weight as he mounted them repeatedly. He became angry now. Raakat should have returned with some prisoners by now. He needed to release his frustration somewhere. His head hurt a lot when he was made to think. If he wasn't beating or killing someone, if he wasn't drinking and if he wasn't defiling yet another woman, then he was thinking, and this was his least favourite activity. He punched the cushion beside him. It burst with a slight 'pow,' and the soft filling from inside flew around before settling on the ground.

Raakat had made the two-night journey to Kamala, the capital city of Karnikapuri. He was aghast when he reached their prisoner encampment. Neither the guards nor the prisoners were around.

He stood for a while, shocked. It was as if his limbs had

been paralyzed, preventing him from moving. Slowly, fear began to creep in. How was he going to tell Moishan about this? He shuddered at the thought. Pictures of a spiked club being aimed at his skull came floating into his mind. No! He could not let Moishan know about this. He looked at the dumb ogre who had gone with him and told him that they had to find out what happened before relaying the news to the master. The tall, bulky man just nodded his head. He was so sluggish and slow that his brain probably couldn't understand more than three words at a time.

Raakat sat down on a makeshift seat that had been used by the prison guards. He had to think about what his next action would be. He did not want to be at the receiving end of Moishan's wrath. That was for sure!

He shuddered at the memory of the last time he had been punished by the brute of a leader. It had been a wet monsoon day, shortly after they entered the lands beyond the icy mountains. Moishan and his army faced, perhaps, the bravest warriors they had ever met. A tribe of people known as the Yavanas clashed with their troops, giving them a tough fight. The leader of the said clan was a well-built young man, heftier than the average man from these parts. The battle was nearing its end, with most of the Yavanas soldiers either dead or gravely wounded. Moishan had just entered into a combat with the leader of the clan. The fight ensued for a long time, neither man being able to shake off or defeat the other. The two had begun to tire, and Moishan suddenly missed a step, causing him to go off balance for a moment. His opponent took this opportunity and drove his sword through the brute's chest. As Moishan fell, the young soldier picked up one of the weapons that Moishan's soldiers had dropped. A club. He began beating Moishan's head to smithereens. Where Moishan got his strength was known only to him, but he suddenly kicked the soldier with all his might, sending him flying into the air. The young soldier fell a few feet away, and Moishan, gathering the last of his strength ripped his heart out with his bare hands before falling unconscious.

He stayed in a comatose state for several weeks. When he finally regained consciousness, he was unable to move his limbs properly for months afterwards. Raakat, who had been Moishan's chief commander and most loyal servant, took care of him and watched over him carefully while he was nursed back to health. Meanwhile, the Buffalo Demon's temporary incapacitation caused small factions within his army to dissent and try to seize power. This included his mindless and ill-advised brothers. Raakat stamped out every dissenting faction and held the barbarian's army together until he was fit to give orders. By now, Moishan's frustration with his condition had turned into maniacal resentment, and he flew into a rage over even the most minor things.

Recognizing that his leader would take a long time to recover, Raakat suggested one day that Moishan should temporarily abandon his quest for power, and they should all return to their homeland. What followed was nothing short of catastrophic for Raakat, and the scars on his back served as constant reminder of that incident.

At Raakat's suggestion, Moishan exploded with rage and ordered his brothers to suspend him from a tree, his arms and legs pulled as far as apart they could be stretched. The pain was excruciating, but it was nothing compared to what was to follow. Moishan told Raakat, 'I want to personally give you a taste of excruciating pain, but as my limbs are useless right now, I will let my brothers do it.'

Moishan signalled to Nishan, whispered something in his ear, and then smiled, his thick lips curling into an evil grin. Nishan took out a sharp dagger and slowly began to slice off layers of skin from Raakat's back. Raakat begged for mercy. The agony and torment made him wish for death. But it was not to be. He stayed suspended with the flesh ripped off his back, blood dripping, for hours. It took every ounce of determination in him not to pass out. He knew that if he lost consciousness, his torment would become worse when he came to. He endured the intense torture until Moishan let him down, not out of compassion or pity, but to keep him as a living example of what happened to anyone who dared to defy, question or oppose him.

Raakat shuddered as the floodgates to the past opened momentarily. His hand involuntarily moved to his back, where several deep scars and gashes ran the length of it, resembling wet sand that had been raked.

He decided now to check the situation in Dwajasthapura with the soldier who had accompanied him, and they rode towards its capital city. Upon reaching the temporary barracks, his heart sank. The prisoners here too had vanished. So had food supplies that were meant for their soldiers. The bloody guards were missing, just like the prisoners. What was he going to do?

'Had our men switched sides? Had they too grown tired of the nomadic life? Did they free the prisoners and go into hiding as well,' he wondered. 'Did the dogs of Saptapuri dare to kill and dispose of his men? If so, where had all the prisoners disappeared?'

He had seen no signs of life anywhere during his ride to Karnikapuri or Dwajasthapura. How had nearly two thousand people just vanished without a trace? He felt so bitter. Raakat kicked hard at the bars of the makeshift prison. It hurt. His toes stung from the impact. But the thought of Moishan's wrath stirred up a much deeper feeling of pain inside the him. He looked at his soldier for any clue as to what was going on beneath that thick skull. Should he ask the soldier to lie to Moishan? If word got out that he had covered up such a big debacle, losing the skin on his back would be the least of his troubles. Raakat closed his eyes for a moment. He had to think. He needed a plan.

'What are you thinking, chief?' mumbled the oaf, standing next to Raakat. In a fit of intense rage, Raakat swung his sword at the soldier, slicing his head off in one clean sweep. He didn't feel one pinch of remorse for his action. His kind had been conditioned not to feel bad or wonder about what was moral or right. They just survived.

Raakat took his time to dig a huge pit. He pushed the headless body into the pit and then kicked the head in. To leave no clue behind, he also shoved the soldier's weapon into the pit. He found some propellant liquid in the stores and set the body on fire. He sat next to it, taking in the repugnant smell of burning flesh. He took out a thin tube from his pocket and filled it with what looked like dried green herbs and lit it. As he slowly took a drag, his muscles relaxed a bit. He smoked away until the body had burned up. Then he filled the pit with the mud he had dug out.

Raakat had decided that, no matter how long it took, he would find a few girls, perhaps from one of the villages surrounding the cities or some tribal settlements that had not been drawn into war. He would attribute his delay to some scuffle he had while bringing the women and pin the death of their soldier on that same incident. Moishan would not mind a fallen soldier if he had the flesh of a woman to prey on.

Reunion at Adiparashakti

Even during their return journey to Pataleshwar fort, Gauri and Shankar diligently meditated and practiced yoga every morning. Gauri had become so particular about her morning routine that she practised alone for three days when Shankar travelled to Dwajasthapura.

On the last day of their journey, just before they crossed over from the Jhoomar forest into the Bhanre forest, the entire battalion was resting. Shankar, who had a keen sixth sense, suddenly motioned to everyone to be silent. He put his ear to the ground, listening intently. Some of the men thought that he had gone mad, but this was a technique that he had learned from Acharya Veni. It was an effective method of determining if someone was approaching. The vibrations of the earth could indicate how they were travelling, approximately what speed they were moving at and their proximity.

He looked up, gathered his soldiers, and said that two horses, each carrying a heavyset man, were approaching at galloping speed and would reach them in approximately forty-five minutes. They had to come up with a plan as they couldn't risk another open conflict with the enemy. A trail of bodies would surely give the enemy an idea of what the Saptapuri men had been up to. They hid all the horses and possessions behind a cluster of trees, a fair distance from the main path that ran through the forest. Two men were to remain with the horses to make sure that they stayed calm. The rest of the men climbed trees and hid themselves in plain sight on either side of the path.

Just as the last of the men had managed to camouflage themselves in the tree's branches, two of Moishan's soldiers on horseback came into view. Shankar recognized the bigger of the two soldiers as someone of importance to Moishan. He had been at the helm of the troops when they first encountered each other on the battlefield. Never had Shankar seen such a cruel face, he thought, as the two men hurriedly passed by. They had not noticed anything and were soon gone. The soldiers waited for a signal from Shankar indicating it was safe to come down. They climbed down the trees, mounted their horses and left at once, lest the two men decide to return or more soldiers follow them on this route.

Shankar and his men were relieved to finally return to Pataleshwar, the underground fort, after a long, tiresome journey. It had been nearly twelve days since they had left the fort. They were also glad that they had lost none of their soldiers during this expedition but had managed to bring back strong and able-bodied men to join their army.

The physically drained people entered the underground fort and collapsed. Vidhushi was elated to see her brother return with so many people in tow. She kissed him on the forehead, and he embraced her.

'How is your student doing?' she whispered into Shankar's ear.

'The student is about to become the master,' he chuckled.

Vidhushi beamed. She warmly welcomed Prince Chandrasekhara and informed him of his mother's success in finding and opening the door to the connecting tunnels. She ensured that he was given a thorough medical check-up and that all scratches and bruises were treated before he could resume his duties. The prince was relieved to know that the rest of the party had moved to the Adiparashakti fortress. He told Shankar that the men should rest for a few hours and then immediately leave for the main fortress to conserve the limited food supply at the underground safe hold. After resting, they gathered their possessions and began walking through the tunnel to the alcove under the Bhanre.

⁂

Meanwhile, Gautami, who had moved to the Adiparashakti fortress, began to worry about her son and all the men who left for Karnikapuri and Dhwajasthipura. It had been nearly twelve days since their departure, and there was no news from them. There was no way to find out if they were safe or if they had been successful in their quest. She brought this up with Pashupati during their meal that evening.

'Should we send a man to find out the whereabouts of our men?' she asked.

'What is the point? We are all going to face the demons soon enough. Let us not waste our resources, Gautami,' said a haggard Pashupati.

'Our boys are being led by the spirited Prince Chandrasekhara and the able-bodied Shankar, who is an embodiment of Mahadeva himself. What is there to worry?' asked Gurupadaka.

They all nodded in agreement and proceeded to finish their dinner.

The following week was one of mass euphoria at the fortress. The rising sun brought with it Chandrasekhara, Shankar, Gauri, and five hundred and thirty young soldiers. There was jubilation all around. Many cheered for their noble king, who had rescued people from other kingdoms. Some were pleased to have additional support as they prepared for the next battle. Others were ecstatic to see their husbands and lovers back, alive and well, from the mission.

Anandamayi's joy knew no bounds when she saw Shankar's serene, glowing face. But her happiness was short-lived when her eyes fell on a dusky woman walking in with Shankar. She was so close to him that their arms brushed against each other. The woman smiled at Anandamayi, but she could hardly return the smile. The muscles in her face tautened, and she clenched her jaws firmly.

'Anandi, meet Gauri,' said Shankar pleasantly. Anandamayi gave a fake smile and folded her hands together to say namaste.

Embraces were being exchanged all around. Gurupadaka held Shankar tightly. Gautami and Indumathi were pulling Chandrasekhara apart, each vying for his affection. The soldiers were tearing away from the gathering to catch up with their loved ones.

From the shadows, Anandamayi observed Gauri, who stood alone, gazing at all the happy faces. She was attempting to size up this woman, this stranger, who seemed important enough for Shankar to know by name and to have personally introduced to her. A hundred questions were raced through Anandamayi's head. She envisioned herself blocking Shankar's path and demanding to know exactly who Gauri was. Her reverie was broken by a gentle tap on her shoulder.

It was Shankar. He embraced her the moment she turned.

'It has been long, my friend,' he said with much courtesy in his voice.

'Let us talk once things settle down a bit today,' he added. Anandamayi's heartbeats began racing. She wondered what he wanted to talk about. Had he missed her? Did he finally realize that she was the one for him? Had he finally understood her affection for him? Did Vidhushi have a hand in this? Her imagination went into overdrive after the warm embrace from Shankar. Suddenly, joy had a new meaning.

The party eventually broke up, and everyone headed back to their respective quarters or their duties. The kitchens needed to be informed that they now had many more mouths to feed. Gautami personally went down to the kitchen to convey this message and to express her gratitude to all the men and women working tirelessly, even in the face of grave, impending danger.

She had always been a wonderful leader. She set reasonable expectations and led by example. She was a leader who walked the talk. If she expected you to be passionate about your work, she showed passion for her own. If she needed you to fight well, she fought well too. She was a beautiful queen, one that the people loved and deserved.

After their morning meal, Pashupati called a meeting of all members of the royal council so that everyone could be brought up to speed on what was happening. All council members were eager to hear about what had occurred at Karnikapuri and Dwajasthapura. Chandrasekhara and Shankar took turns narrating how the events had unfolded. They praised Manikanta, who was at the door, guarding it, and everyone joined in commending the young soldier.

Chandrasekhar also heaped praises on Gauri for how she had handled all the refugees from the other kingdoms, found the underground caves and made them all feel secure in his and Shankar's absence. Gauri blushed, and Pashupati and Gautami beamed. Gurupadaka, Veni and Krishnakanth smiled at Gauri too. Anandamayi alone continued to look down at the table intently.

'I'm sorry, but who is she exactly?' she enquired politely.

It was then that everyone realized that Anandamayi had been at the main fort from the second day of the first battle, and Gauri had only arrived on the third day. The two had never met. Anandamayi was completely unaware of the spectral way Gauri had joined them.

'Gauri is one of us, my dear. The details can be explained later,' said Pashupati, looking at Shankar, who nodded back understandingly. The Maharaja wanted him to fill Anandamayi in on all the details so that the royal council's time would not be wasted.

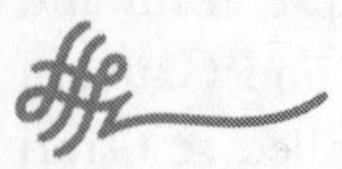

Renewed battle plans

Saptapuri and its allies had just about a month to prepare for its next encounter with the enemy. Battle plans had to be drawn and strategies prepared to face their formidable foe. In the war council meeting, it was decided that the kingdoms of Sahasrara, Dhupghar and Rupghar would mobilize their troops during this period to join the Saptapuri army if a battle ensued with Moishan. Prince Samara of Sangha and King Grehan of Anagraha had gone back to their respective kingdoms along with their troops soon after the first battle. They did not want to strain Amara's meagre resources by staying behind. Since the enemy was too busy burning their dead and counting their losses, both kings had found a safe passage back to their kingdoms. They promised to return with their armies if required.

A decision was also made to send spies to all the kingdoms, informing them of the exact date when they would go to battle again. With the armies of six kingdoms and the prisoners of war rescued from the two fallen kingdoms, they would have a decent number of soldiers. However, this count was still many thousands short of Moishan's demon army. But this time, the war council had a plan. They would take the Ajna Chakra and the Kabali into the battlefield as well.

The Kabali would adopt the battle formation of the sun

and form a Surya Chakra around the sacred stone. These elite warriors would be then protected by Garuda Vyuha, or the eagle formation, positioned ahead of them. The reserve soldiers would position themselves behind the Surya Chakra, placing the sacred stone at the centre of the battle.

The war council hoped that bringing the Ajna Chakra to the battle would draw out the Buffalo Demon to the battlefield, allowing them to kill him. The last time around, Moishan had not entered the theatre of war. So, this time, it was essential to lure him out into the battle arena. The council members believed that once a king or the commander-in-chief of an army is slain, the conflict comes to an end.

The news that the Kabali would be fighting shoulder to shoulder with the rest of the army was the only good thing that Anandamayi had heard the whole morning. It made her straighten her shoulders with pride and finally take her eyes off the table. Her gaze drifted towards Shankar, and in a flash her expression soured when she caught him looking admiringly at the enchantress, Gauri. It took immense restraint on her part not to get up and walk off. Out of respect for all the royals at the table, she remained seated but returned her gaze to the table once more.

After the meeting was over, and even before the council could disperse, Anandamayi speedily left the hall and began walking towards her room. She heard footsteps behind her and she quickened her pace, sensing that Shankar wanted to talk. She wanted to avoid this right now, as she realized that nothing good would come of it. She had seen in Shankar's eyes an admiration for Gauri, one that she had never seen in his eyes for anyone else before.

As she had anticipated, he caught up with her a moment

later and said, 'Anandi, can you spare a little of your time now? We can take a walk together.' Anandamayi grunted in a non-committal way. They began walking towards the stairs that led to one of the turrets of the fort. Soon, they were taking a stroll under the sun.

'Anandi, you are aware of the prophecy on the temple wall. It speaks of a great evil that would endanger the existence of Saptapuri and of a goddess who would appear to rid us of this danger. I believe that Gauri is the answer.' He then went on to recount how Gauri had appeared out of nowhere during the battle, how she got hurt and her crucial role in the rescue operation.

Anandamayi threw Shankar a look of pure contempt after hearing what he had said. She was a fierce, outspoken woman and expressed her anger and disbelief openly. 'What is wrong with every single one of you? Are you all blind? In what way does this woman look like a goddess to you? Everything that drops out of the sky isn't celestial. She is not going to rescue us. You have your hopes pinned on the wrong person and you are going to be sorry for trusting her.'

'Do not expect me to be a willing part of this sham you all have going on here. I would rather be realistic and focus on battle tactics to save our kingdom. Now, if that is all, I have better things to do. See you around, Shankar.'

She turned around and began walking away. 'Anandi, wait,' said Shankar, catching hold of her hand tightly. She twisted it out of his grasp in anger and glared at him.

'What?'

'I need a favour from you. You specialize in one-to-one combat, the use of weaponry and are an excellent warrior. You are the best teacher that we have seen so far.'

'Get to the point, sir,' she said with impatience.

'I request you to teach Gauri the use of weapons and help her gain mastery over duelling and other forms of combat.'

Anandamayi laughed sarcastically and said, 'Your goddess doesn't know how to fight? This is getting interesting.'

'Anandi, you need not believe or have faith in the prophecy. But you are a good teacher, and I would entrust no other with this task. Please say you will teach Gauri. We have little time, and I need all the help I can get.' Shankar's voice had gone from its usual polite, steady tone to one of pleading. This caught Anandamayi off guard. She had never seen Shankar vexed about anything. Even in the face of trouble, Shankar had always been calm and composed.

She looked at her friend, feeling a tinge of sympathy for him. 'Fine but remember that I am doing this only for you. You owe me.'

'I'll always be indebted to you, Anandi,' he replied with a sigh of relief.

'There is not enough open space here to teach her the art of combat, nor can she learn how to use a sword, bow and arrow or any weapon for that matter. How do you plan to address the space problem?' questioned Anandamayi.

'The training centre for the Kabali is a few miles from here. There have been no signs of trouble or sightings of the enemy until now. We can ride out there every morning so she can learn. We will, of course, have to be discreet as well as prudent about it.'

'We begin at sunrise tomorrow then,' said Anandamayi.

'Please come to the centre at sunrise. Both of us will meet you there. Until sunrise, she is will undergo physical and psychological wellness training with me.'

Hearing this, Anandamayi's heart sank lower than she thought possible. Shankar had considered Gauri to be special enough to give her his undivided attention and take a personal interest in her training. For the first time in her life, Anadamayi felt like she was losing Shankar.

The training

Anandamayi left for the training centre just before sunrise. It would take her less than half an hour to get there. She reached just in time to see Shankar and Gauri stirring from their deep meditation. They were seated facing each other as guru and shishya usually would. She waited until they opened their eyes. When Shankar saw her, he smiled and greeted her.

He looked at Gauri and said, 'Gauri, you have met Anandamayi. She is an exceptional teacher and a master warrior. As I mentioned earlier, she will train you in the use of weapons, the art of combat, archery and any other skills that would be useful on the battlefield. You have little time to master these skills. If you wish to join the battle, you must not be a bane; you must be our blessing.'

Gauri nodded, looking unsure and sceptical. She was determined, after the last few days of adventure, that she wanted to contribute. She didn't want to be seated on the sidelines while the rest fought the Buffalo Demon.

The training centre was known as Bajarang Baan, named after the fearless monkey god, Hanuman. It was a walled, circular campus spread over an acre. The only entrance was through a heavy metal gate that faced the path leading to Lake Pravasi. As soon as one entered, one was greeted by a humungous banyan tree, its roots and branches spreading out and covering several feet of ground. There was a platform that went around the trunk of the tree, on which stood the statue of a fierce-looking Ma Kaali. She was adorned in blood-red garments and bedecked with stone jewellery. Each of her eight arms held a weapon. The foremost arms held a trishul and an axe. The second set of arms held a sword and shield. A third set of arms held a bow with arrows, and the uppermost arms held a discus and fire.

Moving past the tree, one saw a large square platform three feet off the ground. It was plain, with steps at the centre of each side of the square leading up to the platform. This platform occupied a large part of space and was intended for combat training. Beyond the platform, one could see dedicated, small, partitioned areas meant for training wrestlers, sword fighters and mace users.

Running parallel to the wall on the left side of the entrance was a row of small huts where the trainees stayed. There was a long dining hall at the end of the row of huts, followed by a massive kitchen area. On the opposite side, there were two circular rooms, which housed an assortment of different weapons. A portion of the open space was designated for practicing archery and spear-throwing.

The boundary of the entire training camp was lined with tall trees to block outsiders from seeing what was happening inside the Bajarang Baan. Some of these trees had small plinth-like structures beside them for meditation. The training camp was a self-sufficient complex, complete with baths, water tanks and prayer halls to meet the needs of the Kabali students.

Once a person was selected for training and entered Bajarang Baan, they only stepped out into the real world after joining the esteemed ranks of the Kabali fighters. People had spent their entire childhood and young adult years within the boundaries of Bajarang Baan along with their teachers and other students. They never ventured far from the training camp, perhaps only going as far as Lake Pravasi, but never beyond.

Gauri began her training with Anandamayi under the watchful eyes of Shankar. The first few days were very painful and embarrassing for Gauri. Yet every day, she woke up and made renewed efforts. Her body, which was not used to the rigour of carrying and wielding weapons, became sore to the point where she couldn't even breathe without pain. Her muscles became stiff, leaving her unable to move freely once the training for the day was done. Even coughing became an effort, as her diaphragm hurt and her eyes watered from the pain. But she would not relent. Every day she pushed herself harder because of Shankar's immense faith in her. She could not let him down. She did not know what role she was going to play in the impending war, but she had to learn how to brandish a sword or wield a dagger. She also needed to learn how to tactically manoeuvre through a battlefield without getting herself killed.

How far Gauri had come: from being a meek scientist in a laboratory in Bengaluru to a girl learning how to use weapons in a completely different world from a different era. Gauri was still having disturbing dreams, but this time they were about her family and friends back home. She missed them like crazy. Her heart ached like somebody was crushing it, but her mind was resilient. She did not want to give up and break Shankar's trust. She didn't understand why this was so important to her now, but he felt like family, and he was the only person she felt affectionate towards.

Anandamayi hated her new student. She was a mean and tough taskmaster. She never allowed Gauri to take a break or rest, even when she was tired. She threw a new weapon at Gauri every day and came down hard on her. She hit hard, she attacked fiercely and she defended like a tigress. But even she had to respect Gauri's sheer grit and willpower. She was also surprised and taken aback at how well Gauri learned. She learned the art of one-to-one combat in under seven days and began sharpening her form and technique steadily.

Slowly, Shankar stopped going with them to their early morning sessions. Anandamayi continued to teach sincerely. She didn't agree completely with the war council's vision, but she didn't let it interfere with her teaching. She would never compromise her values as a warrior and a teacher. The student and the teacher barely exchanged any words during their classes, and no interaction took place between them when they returned to Adiparashakti each day after training.

Gauri had realized that Anandamayi disliked her, and she did not know why. However, she treated her teacher with utmost respect.

Anandamayi had nothing but jealousy and hate in her heart for Gauri. She had never seen Gauri say or do anything that deserved this, but she couldn't tolerate the attention Gauri received from everybody, especially Shankar. This jealousy consumed her and she could not stand to be in the same room as both Shankar and Gauri. While the people around them were oblivious, Anandamayi could clearly see that Shankar had eyes for no one other than Gauri.

A few days into their training, Gauri approached Anandamayi and said, 'You are the finest teacher I have had since my childhood. I want to pay my respects to you by way of *gurudakshina*. Please allow me to do so by accepting my humble offering.' She opened her clasped palm to offer Anandamayi a golden bracelet with tiny charms dangling from the central circle.

'I do not need your gurudakshina,' said an offended Anandamayi. She contorted her face in disgust. Withdrawing her bracelet, Gauri said gently, 'But you must allow me to pay my respects for everything you have taught me.

Anandamayi looked straight into Gauri's eyes, trying to discern if she was being truly respectful. Once she recognized Gauri's sincere effort, her attitude softened a bit. She realized that what she genuinely wanted from Gauri was for her to stay away from Shankar. Even in her own mind, Anandamayi realized how unreasonable she was being, but the pain and fear of losing Shankar outweighed everything else. She looked away, holding back a tear as she tried to find her voice. She finally managed to look at Gauri and say, 'I'll ask for gurudakshina when the time comes. But you must promise to honour my request.'

'I most certainly will,' said Gauri, politely.

Slaying a demon

Raakat was tired and at his wit's end. He had been riding for nearly fifteen days, trying to find women to take back to Moishan. What was he going to do? There was no honour in killing himself. He could have done that several years ago. Why put up with so much of Moishan's brutality? There was certainly no sense in going back without a prey for his brutal lord. His back couldn't take another skinning. He wasn't as strong or as young as he had been before.

He mindlessly rode his horse towards Lake Pravasi, located a few miles beyond the city limits, where Moishan had camped. He needed to drink some water and think about his options. He stopped at the lake and tied his horse to a nearby tree. He drank his fill of water and splashed his head and face to cool himself down. He lay down on the grass and closed his eyes for a moment when he heard voices in the distance. They sounded like female voices, but he couldn't be sure. He wondered if luck had finally come his way.

Raakat quietly and cautiously walked towards the voices. He peeped over the high wall and saw two women. One was instructing the other on the use of a short-blade dagger. The place looked like a deserted school for performing arts or some such thing. Raakat held himself steady and watched for a while.

It had been an unusually hot morning. The sun was blazing fiercely. Anandamayi could feel her skin burning and beads of sweat ran down her forehead and cheeks. She wiped it off with a stroke of her left hand as she continued to duel with Gauri. Even Gauri's clothes were wet from sweating profusely. Her hair which had been plaited back was wet, dishevelled and almost completely undone.

'How stubborn and unrelenting is this girl,' Anandamayi thought to herself. The heat was making her irritable, and she was taking it out on Gauri. Every move of hers was fierce and premeditated, hoping to make Gauri give up.

She wanted Gauri to throw down her weapons and declare, 'I'm done. This isn't for me,' But Gauri seemed to be in no mood to oblige. She was fighting back like a tigress. Every counterblow felt as if she was unleashing her vengeance on something.

Anandamayi finally gave up. The heat was getting to her. Gauri's stubbornness was making her angry as well. She needed to cool off. She needed water. But all the stored water at Bajrang Baan had dried up.

'That's enough.' She shouted to Gauri, throwing down her weapon.

'Meditate for a while. I am going to the lake to fetch some water. You need to build more focus through meditation. You are distracted easily,' she told Gauri spitefully. Gauri simply nodded in return.

Raakat smiled. Luck was on his side. Not that he had any problem dealing with two puny women. The dumb broads were out alone, playing with weapons. This was no place for them anyway. Their place was under a man. He rubbed his palms together and waited for the first woman to leave. He would get her too when she came back.

Gauri sat down to meditate. She was glad to have a break. This was the first time that Anandamayi had relented and given Gauri one. Even though her body had grown used to the intense physical activity, she still hoped for a respite now and then. She closed her eyes, took deep breaths and steadied her rapid heartbeat.

As her focus intensified, she became aware of her surroundings, the stillness of the air and the silence. A few minutes had passed when the stillness was broken by a very slight movement. Gauri sensed an ever-so-subtle change in the environment. The air smelt a little different. Gauri opened her eyes, wondering if Anandamayi had returned. But she did not see her.

Gauri decided to explore the training centre instead of meditating. She realized that she might not get another chance to check out the place once Anandamayi returned. She took a walk on the raised central platform and then jumped off, heading toward the rooms where weapons had been stored. She wondered if there were still any weapons left behind? She entered the room. It was dark and cool. It took some time for Gauri's eyes to adjust to the darkness. She noticed that the room was empty. When the city was evacuated, so was the Bajrang Baan. There was, however, a sword lying in the middle of the room. It must have been left behind somehow. Gauri went and picked it up. It was a beautifully crafted piece. With her practice sword, she couldn't quite cut a fruit even if she wanted to. Gauri carried out this magnificent weapon, thinking she could practice her moves with it until Anandamayi came back. She stepped out of the dark room and walked back to her training area.

As she reached the area, she was aghast to see a monstrous

form hulking towards her. The warrior was tall, taller than six feet. His bushy hair was tied in a long ponytail at the top of his head. He was bare-chested except for an assortment of beads strung around his neck. His ear lobes were pierced and from each of them hung a roughly cut black rock, held together and fastened by a wire. Below his waist, he wore a black dhoti-like garment that was broad and ruffled at the thighs, narrowing as it went down and bunched around his calf muscles before disappearing into his large boots. His body was scarred in several places. There was a deep gash across his left eyebrow that made him look particularly evil.

Gauri stopped in her tracks, her body becoming tense at once. She pointed the sword in her hand at the strange-looking monster and glowered. 'Stay where you are, do not come forward.'

The huge brute stopped for a moment, looking amused. As he smiled, she noticed that his teeth were broken and stained brown. She realized that he didn't understand her words but was mocking her based on his body language. He looked at Gauri menacingly and barked something in a strange tongue. Gauri was gripped with fear and felt a twister brewing in the pit of her stomach. Her only thought was whether she could stall this monster until Anandamayi returned? The beast had begun inching towards her again. She waved her sword like a lunatic. He let out a chuckle. His laughter echoed in the stillness of the air. Gauri steadied herself and put her right foot forward, with her left foot positioned perpendicularly behind it. Her left arm was raised above her head for better balance, and her right arm came forward with the sword. Her stance resembled that of a seasoned warrior, although she didn't feel like one.

Anandamayi had barely reached the lake when she saw a

horse tied to a tree and instantly knew something was amiss. She sprinted back to the training centre, only to see the back of a gigantic, barbaric-looking soldier inching towards Gauri.

Out of the corner of her eye, Gauri saw movement behind the massive warrior. She thanked her stars that Anandamayi had returned. However, she didn't break her stance and continued to look at the brute intently.

Suddenly, he swung around and lunged towards Anandamayi. He grabbed her by her throat and lifted her off the ground. Anandamayi tried to punch him but was unable connect; the man was so big that the arm by which he had caught her extended far in front of him and her arm was far too short to reach him. Suspended in the air, she began to choke but fought hard to loosen his grip around her throat. She wheezed at him between breaths. 'Fight like a man. Put me down.' She was barely audible, and her face was turning blue. The brute was taking pleasure in strangling her. His beady eyes held a strange sense of satisfaction as he held the flailing form in the air.

Even through her breathless tussle, Anandamayi was trying to encourage Gauri to step forward and attack the man. Gauri couldn't move. She was frozen in her place. Paralyzed!

The man, without warning, flung Anandamayi to the ground with full force. She landed head-first on a step that led to the practice arena. Her head began to bleed, but the colour on her face slowly returned as she could now breathe.

Seeing Anandamayi being flung like a carcass, ignited something inside Gauri. She moved at lightning speed, picked up a shield and went running to attack the barbarian. He removed his sword from its hilt and countered her. He was strong, and she buckled under his counterattack. She was on one knee now, using the shield to defend herself against his blows with one hand and using her sword to counter his attacks with the other. However, she was much shorter and swifter than he was. She used her agility and her short stature to her advantage, quickly flipping backwards to get back on her feet between blows. Raakat smiled in surprise at her nimbleness. Suddenly he began chanting, 'Raakat, Raakat,' while pointing at himself. It was as if he was enjoying some sport in an arena and cheering on his favourite.

Raakat was enraged. No woman had ever dared to pick up a weapon to oppose him, and his ego was tremendously hurt. At first, he wanted to blow Gauri's head open, but then realized that he had to bring both women back alive to Moishan. For a moment, he had forgotten that he couldn't kill these two women.

Anandamayi was bleeding profusely now. She tried getting up to help Gauri but her knees buckled. She fell again and looked towards Gauri. The girl was locked in a sword fight with the madman chanting what appeared to be his own name. She had lasted long for a first-time fighter. Anandamayi was rueful that Shankar had stopped joining them during training. She made one last effort to stand to help Gauri. But what she saw made her catch her breath. Gauri's eyes were glowering in rage, and she was exuding an energy that was striking. There seemed to be a sudden surge of power in her movements.

Gauri elegantly ducked the barbarian's sword and took a clean stab at his heart. He fell to his knees, looking up at the face that had put a sword into him. His eyes filled up with tears, and his face looked surprisingly peaceful. He looked as if he had been delivered from a laborious and wicked life. Blood began oozing out from where the sword had entered. Gauri kicked his chest forcefully while simultaneously slashing her sword across his neck, cutting his head off in a neat sweep. She bellowed at him, strong words that would ring in Anandamayi's ears for a long time to come.

'Your blood shall not taint these lands again, Raakat!'

Gauri lifted his head with the tip of her sword, letting the blood from the severed head drip down onto her shield beneath. It was a remarkable sight—terrifying yet satisfying. Anandamayi closed her eyes, slipping into unconsciousness.

Next, when she opened her eyes, she found herself lying on a bed. Everything around her appeared hazy and blurry. 'Keep your eyes closed,' commanded a voice that she was familiar with and had missed much over the last few days. Vidhushi had been summoned from the underground fortress. She was sent a note written on a parchment. It simply read, 'Please come at once. It's an emergency.' Vidhushi rushed to the main fort with all kinds of horrible images racing through her mind. She envisioned the worst possible scenario for every member of the royal family.

The only person who didn't flash through her mind was her brother. Shankar seemed incapable of getting hurt or being in trouble. Vidhushi couldn't recall a single day since they met when he had fallen ill—not a cough, not high temperature, not an infection, nothing at all. Remarkably, he had not even been physically injured once. She had never seen him bleed. Strange as it was, she had never been perplexed by it. Her thoughts were focused on the Maharani Gautami, Maharaja Pashupati, their royal guest Raja Krishnakanth and even the mysterious Gauri.

On reaching the fort, Vidhushi had been led to an unconscious Anandamayi, whose forehead was split open and who had lost a lot of blood. However, her wound had been cleaned and some kind of paste had been applied to it. Vidhushi lightly picked up a bit of the salve between her forefinger and thumb and smelled it. Seeming satisfied, she automatically looked at Shankar and nodded. She assured everyone that Anandamayi would be fine in a matter of four nights and there was nothing to worry about.

Gurupadaka explained to Vidhushi that Gauri and Anandamayi were attacked by a mercenary of Moishan's army while they were training at Bajarang Ban. Anandamayi got hurt while fighting the mercenary. Nobody until now had heard the unabridged and whole truth about what had happened that day.

Gauri had returned that day riding back with an unconscious Anandamayi. Her clothes were soaked in blood, and her eyes were scarlet. She muttered something incoherently about being attacked, at which point Shankar and Gurupadaka relieved her of Anandamayi's limp body. One of the chamberlains held Gauri's hand and led her away to help calm her down. In the meantime, Shankar had cleaned and dressed Anandamayi's wound using the knowledge he had gained growing up with Vidhushi. Word had been sent to Vidhushi to come to the fort at once. Once Anandamayi had been adequately taken care of, they approached a bewildered Gauri to ask her what had happened.

Gauri had behaved very strangely that day. She broke down into tears when asked about what had happened. Through her sobbing, all they understood was that the women were attacked by someone called Raakat, who was now dead, and that Anandamayi was hurt during the fight. The explanation seemed somewhat sufficient at that point, so they chose not to distress Gauri by questioning her any further. They decided to leave her alone.

Anandamayi, eyes still closed, asked Vidhushi, who was constantly by her side, 'How long have I been out?'

'Four days,' came the reply.

'Why can't I open my eyes yet?'

'You may open them, but your vision will be blurred for a few days. The blow to your head was so severe that it has impacted your vision. Also, you have been swimming in and out of consciousness. You may experience some memory loss as well, from what I have observed over the past two days since I got here.'

'Gauri?' she enquired in a curious tone.

'She has been visiting you every day. She was here first thing this morning as well. She just sits here silently, cries and then leaves.'

'What about her training?'

'She has been practicing. Gurupadaka and Shankar go with her during the early hours of the morning.'

'Did she say what happened that day?'

'I think you should get some rest, Anandi. The biggest war ever is at our doorstep. You have to recover fully to put up a good fight.'

It took nine more days for Anandamayi's vision to be completely restored. She had made a full recovery and had begun watching Gauri practice all that she had learnt so far. She had even gained enough strength to teach the girl some swift manoeuvres to avoid arrows and other weapons on the field. The two women were still not chatty, but there was a newfound respect for Gauri in Anandamayi's eyes. She had even started to smile at Gauri occasionally. Gauri too had stopped crying now that Anandamayi was out of danger. Everyone assumed that she had been afraid for Anandamayi's life and that the attack had unhinged her.

Since the day she killed Raakat, Gauri had become withdrawn and cried easily. Everyone believed this was the effect of the unexpected attack. Neither did she tell anyone who had killed Raakat, nor did she have the nerve to describe how it had been done. Gauri shuddered each time she recalled the events of the day. What had gotten into her? It felt as though she had been possessed. She had stabbed the beast through his heart and then severed his head while he watched her do it. It was almost like she didn't know who she was anymore.

She had made up her mind that she somehow had to find her way back to her world. She missed Ananya so much. Her best friend would have known how to calm her down. Ananya had a way with words. She was funny and her sense of humour dissipated any tension in the air. Here, Gauri didn't have a shoulder to lean on. Everyone was respectful and kind to her, but she still felt out of place in this foreign land. She felt isolated and completely alone.

Gauri continued her practices. Meditation calmed her down, improved her energy levels and gave her a sense of peace. Combat training kept her occupied and provided an outlet to expend all the extra energy she had gained through intense physical training and meditation.

Once she was through with her training for the day, she shut herself in her small room. She started experimenting with the chemicals she had carried back from Karnikapuri. Each day, she attempted a different combination, trying to recreate the volatile liquid that had caused her dislocation on that fateful day. But nothing seemed to work. She set aside each liquid she distilled, throwing away nothing, in the hope that one of them would have an unexpected reaction that could take her back. She had become secretive and reclusive, not wanting any interference with what she was doing. If her experiments didn't work, and she remained trapped in this realm, she would learn to adjust. But if luck favoured her and she could return, she would have her life back.

Shortly after Anandamayi's recovery, the fort was abuzz with talk that Gauri was the one who killed Raakat. There were multiple versions of how she had cut off his head. Tall tales were afloat about how she had danced in a frenzy around the slain demon and how there was a spectral aura around her. People looked at Gauri with renewed reverence.

The royals, Gurupadaka, and Vidhushi looked at Gauri with newfound hope and respect when she joined them during mealtimes. Shankar alone remained unaffected by Anandamayi's accounts. He had been waiting for something like this to happen ever since Gauri had arrived. She was indeed Kali! Meanwhile, Anandamayi tried to quell the gossip surrounding the incident. 'The warrior was of this earth. Gauri is of this earth, and she killed him like any warrior would. Stop spreading tales.'

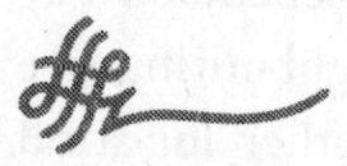

A search for Raakat

Bhugol was a senior minister in Maharaja Pashupati's cabinet. He had been a loyal member of the king's staff for nearly thirty years. Ever since he was a young lad, he had aspired to become a minister in the king's cabinet. While growing up, he had observed various ministers coming and going from the palace, often discussing trade, welfare measures or new policies aimed at improving the lives of the people. Bhugol wanted to be like them. He wanted to grow up and do something significant and lasting for the people so that they would always remember him. He sought to emulate Pashupati and be a model citizen.

Bhugol had a unique value system. He never viewed any issue as strictly right or wrong or black or white. He firmly believed that the interpretation of facts was dependent on individual perspectives and the context. For instance, when it came to petty crimes, he offered the benefit of the doubt to those involved. He sought to understand the background of the crime, and what emotions and life situations that led to it, rather than solely focusing on the act itself. The cabinet of ministers found this approach rather radical. Some criticized him for it, while others admired him. Yet, he had risen to become the senior-most minister by the time he was thirty years old. Now, at the age of fifty, he was well-respected and loved by the younger ministers.

With just twenty days remaining until the scheduled day of battle, Bhugol was tasked to travel to the neighbouring five kingdoms to notify them about the date and other logistical details. He was instructed to inform the kings of the respective kingdoms that they were expected to gather outside Amara two days prior to the big day to discuss battle strategies and formations.

The long, circuitous journey had to be carefully planned to ensure Bhugol's return to Amara five days before the battle. The minister intended to ride around Lake Pravasi to first reach the kingdom of Rupghar. From there, he would proceed towards the kingdoms of Dhupghar and Sahasrara. After covering those, he would travel to Sangha, a kingdom further down south, cutting through the kingdom of Karpura. Next, he would ride southwest towards his last destination, the kingdom of Anagraha. After delivering all the messages, he would then journey north to return home, arriving near Lake Pravasi.

Bhugol paid obeisance to the Royals and left on his mission.

A fly was incessantly buzzing around, repeatedly appearing at the table. Each time Moishan waved his hand around to shoo the little creature, his irritation grew. He was devouring the meat in front of him like a beast tearing the carcass off its prey after a hunt. He was angry that he had been idle for nearly a month, and to add to his woes, there was no sign of Raakat.

It had been nearly twenty days since Raakat had left with one soldier in tow to find women for him. Moishan didn't quite feel right about this. Something was irking him about Raakat's disappearance. The old man had been faithful to him through all his conquests, brutalities and misadventures. Surely, he hadn't just run off on a whim. Besides, who was there to run to? They were surrounded by pathetic creatures who held a weapon of immense power and yet were hiding like meek little rodents. They deserved to be squashed to a pulp, and surely Raakat wouldn't dare to join hands with such cowards.

The Buffalo Demon decided to send his men to find Raakat or find out what happened to him. He wasn't worried, and he certainly wasn't attached to Raakat. He was just bored and needed to do something.

He called out to his brothers, Shumran and Nishan. The two had nearly finished all the intoxicants that the city's brewery had to offer. Eternally drunk and inept at almost everything, the only reason these two idiots were alive was because they served well as muscle men and executed thuggish tasks that didn't require application of the mind. Moishan instructed them to fetch three lieutenants who were close to Raakat.

This task alone took the two oafs a few hours. Once the three men had been found, they were instructed to meet Moishan in his tent. The three lieutenants wondered what horror awaited them. But having no choice, they went as summoned. Moishan was not his usual self. He was distracted. He was contemplative. He was making use of his brain.

'Do any of you know where Raakat went?'

'No, my lord,' said Yonga.

'Neither do I,' said Simrik.

'I believe he took Khara and went to the cities we had laid to waste to bring all the female prisoners back here, my lord,' said Songhiu.

'Hmm... You will now retrace his path and find him. He has been away for far too long.'

'Certainly, my lord,' the three said in unison.

'Then be gone and do not return without Raakat.'

Songhiu, Yonga, and Simrik set off immediately. Their first stop at the capital city of Karnikapuri sent them into a state of frenzied shock. Nothing remained of their outpost. The three young men were worried. Their leader would not be pleased with this news. They decided to ride to Dwajasthapura before reaching any conclusions. Upon arrival, they discovered that it was deserted as well. There was no garrison, no prisoners and no soldiers. There was no sign of Raakat either.

'Search everywhere, until you find something that can point us in the right direction. We need some clue or sign of what we are dealing with,' said Yonga.

They split up to explore the area to figure out what had happened when Simrik shouted out to the other two. They came running to him. He pointed at the ground beneath them. It looked as if it had been recently dug up and filled back in. The men knew that it meant something. They began digging the place for answers. The summer heat was scorching, roasting them like pigs on a spit. But they continued their task; they needed answers. They kept digging until they caught a sickly acrid smell of rotting, burnt flesh. It was disgusting and sent the three of them into a swirling stupor. They backed away at once. All three of them tore pieces of cloth that they could scavenge from the surroundings and tied them around their noses. They dug a bit further. What they found left them utterly stupefied. It was the remains of Khara's body. They were only able to identify the necrotic remains because of the massive, spiked club that was buried with the body. It had a silken ribbon tied around it, which they knew he used on all his weapons to bring him luck.

The three men felt faint from digging under the blazing sun and from what they had uncovered. Who had killed Khara, they wondered.

'If Khara is dead, where is Raakat?' asked Yonga.

'Also, where are all the prisoners and soldiers from this outpost?' mumbled Songhiu.

'Should we check around the garrison?' Yonga wondered aloud.

'Yes, we should,' said Simrik. 'Let us explore the outskirts of all the conquered cities for any sign of life and clues about Raakat.'

The three soldiers began to have a sinking feeling.

'I am scared to return to our camp,' said Yonga. 'Our leader will skin us alive when he hears about all this.'

'We didn't do anything. We are just relaying facts,' said Simrik, trying to sound brave.

'So was that poor bastard who told Moishan a few days ago that some of our soldiers were found dead in the forest bordering Karnikapuri. He ended up getting his head smashed and his stomach kicked so hard that he never stood up again,' recounted Songhiu.

'Ok, what else can we do? Should we run away because we have shocking news to convey. That is just stupid. Lord Moishan is ill-tempered, but he is our leader. We fear him as we revere him. We serve him because he is a fearless leader. He will rule the world one day. And we will be rewarded for being by his side then,' said Simrik loftily.

'You are right. Let us run a perimeter check of all three cities and go back to Lord Moishan with the news,' said Yonga.

Two days later, they rode back to the outskirts of Amara, where their troops were camped. They knew a massive lake lay just beyond. They decided to ride along the banks of the lake and its adjoining lands one last time before returning to their camp. As they rode towards the lake, they were surprised to see a lone horse cantering past them. It had no rider, but it was saddled exactly as their horses had been. They gave chase and caught up to it after some distance.

They surrounded the horse on three sides. The animal showed signs of aggression. Its ears were flattened backwards and its lips were curled back. It kept snaking and pawing the ground, not allowing them to come close. The animal also squealed, bowed its head and continued rearing with its hindquarters deeply flexed, as if threatening to kick. They captured the horse with much difficulty. Upon examining the animal, they concluded that it must have been the Raakat's horse. This gave them some hope, and they began scouring the nearby area for any sign of Raakat.

What they came across next sent a chill down their spines. They found Raakat. Well, they found his body! His head and body lay a few feet apart. The place looked like a desolate camp.

All three men had different theories as to what might have transpired. One guessed that whoever freed the prisoners killed Khara and subsequently chased down Rakat and killed him too.

Another one wondered why was Khara's body was burnt and buried while all the other bodies were found in the open. The only thing they agreed on was that they should bag Raakat's head and carry it along as proof for Lord Moishan to see.

After bagging the head, they went down to the river for a drink. As they sat on the riverbank, they could see dust rising in the distance. A lone rider was riding in their direction. From his attire, he appeared to be a subject of the Saptapuri kingdom. The three young barbarians hid themselves and waited for the rider to come closer. They sprang out from three sides to accost the rider. They pulled him off his horse, and Yonga grabbed him by his throat.

Bhugol, who was returning after delivering messages to all the kingdoms, was petrified and nearly died of a heart attack when the three savages from Moishan's army captured him. As one of them held his throat and forced him down onto his knees, they began barking at each other in their language.

'We can ask him what has been going on. He can explain what happened to our prisoners, Khara and Raakat too. Once he reveals the information, we can finish him off and convey the news to Lord Moishan,' said Yonga.

'Let us not waste time. How do you know he knows anything?' Simrik countered Yonga.

Songhiu suggested, 'Let us take him back to Lord Moishan and conduct our investigation there. He can decide what needs to be done with him. If he is preoccupied with bludgeoning him to death, then we might escape the brunt of his anger over the undesirable events. This man could serve as our scapegoat.'

'You are a fool. How would we even get him to talk? Do any of us understand his language?' Simrik retorted angrily. He was beginning to get aggressive.

Out of the three young men, Songhiu had developed conversational skills in the local language. He managed pick up a bit of the local tongue in every kingdom they conquered by speaking and listening to the prisoners of war. He had never disclosed this ability to anyone because he feared he would have been ridiculed and picked on by his fellow soldiers. He now sheepishly looked at them and said, 'I can speak their tongue.'

After his comrades' stunned reactions, the three of them gagged the prisoner, tied him to Raakat's horse and made their way back to their camp in Amara.

The weight of choices

Tensions were mounting within the fort as the day of the battle approached. The king, the prince, the soldiers and everyone else were fully immersed in preparing for war.

Anandamayi and Gauri would be among the few women on the battlefield. Most of the women who were going to fight were enlisted in the Kabali and would be part of the core Surya chakra formation.

The other women were growing anxious about letting their men go off to war again. The children, however, were shielded from all the anxiety by engaging them in play and study. Tanmay, the son of Crown Prince Chandrasekhara, was also sent to mingle and play with the other children. To ensure the children didn't become cranky and restless from being cooped up inside the fortress, Rajguru Dhumbaka and Acharya Veni were tasked with tutoring them. This kept them occupied and prevented any disruption in their education. The children were engaged in physical activities that helped expend their pent-up energy, ensuring that they didn't come in the way of the men preparing for battle.

Bhugol woke up in a room filled with smoke. He recognized the smell as that of weed smoked by devotees of Veerabhadra and Kalabhairava, the more ferocious and darker manifestations of Lord Shambho Mahadev! As he looked around, he noticed the three vicious youths who had waylaid him. They were standing in front of a throne. The ends of each arm of the throne were carved with the face of a fierce-looking buffalo with gigantic, thick horns protruding from its head. On it sat the meanest, largest monster that Bhugol had ever laid eyes on. He gulped, realizing who he was facing. Closing his eyes he began muttering prayers to Lord Shiva and Ma Shakti to save him from this perilous and grave situation.

A loud crack of a whip made Bhugol open his eyes. The face of the Buffalo Demon resembled that of Yama, the lord of death. He held the whip with sharp spikes in his hand. The front end of the whip had a double-ended hook knotted to it, and the back end had a thick handle for holding.

Bhugol's eyes glazed over as they fixated on the horns of the buffalo engraved on the chair. He was sweating profusely, and beads of sweat were rolling down the side of his face, dripping onto the *angavastra* that adorned his upper body. Blood had rushed to his face and his head was throbbing. His heart was pounding so hard it felt like it would break his ribs. Bhugol had never thought that he would face his death in such an unexpected and undesirable manner.

One of the three soldiers spoke up, addressing the frightening giant on the throne. His gnarled voice addressed the giant as Moishan and said something to him. Moishan made some loud barking noises that sent a chill down Bhugol's spine. He thought he might just die of fear. The other two soldiers then took turns to explain something to Moishan. They opened a bag that they carried and let something roll out. Bhugol's blood curdled when he saw a decapitated head rolling out onto the floor, coming to rest two feet from where he was lying. He began to wheeze at the sight of the head, but a thunderous roar from Moishan silenced him completely.

The demon king bellowed as if the head were his own. It was not a scream caused by pain; it was a scream that signified rage and pure hatred.

Moishan was enraged on seeing Raakat's head on the floor. He wanted to rip out the heart of the man lying on the floor. He picked up his club and menacingly stepped forward towards Bhugol when the smallest of the three men ran to Moishan, knelt in his path, and said something that made Moishan stop.

Moishan frowned deeply, almost contorting his face, and thought for a while. He then nodded at the fellow whom he addressed as Songhiu.

Songhiu turned to Bhugol and asked, 'Where are the people of Saptapuri hiding?'

Bhugol was taken aback. One of them could speak his language. He hesitated. He couldn't give away the secrets of his kingdom to these mercenaries. His soul wouldn't find a place in heaven if he betrayed an entire kingdom. He shook his head helplessly from side to side, feigning ignorance. Songhiu repeated the question. Bhugol shook his head again.

The whip came cracking down, and the metal hook scraped the floor an inch away from Bhugol's knees. His eyes widened further with fear. But his resolve didn't change.

Moishan said something to Songhiu, and the three men bent down and dragged a bound Bhugol out of the smoke-filled tent. Outside, they began beating him mercilessly while Songhiu kept questioning him. Where were the people hiding? What happened to the prisoners from Karnikapuri and Dwajasthapura? Who killed Khara and Raakat? What was the plan of the king now?

Bhugol said nothing. He was resolute. He would rather die at their hands than endanger the lives of thousands of innocent people.

The men were pounding and smacking Bhugol without mercy when Moishan summoned them. They left Bhugol lying on the ground severely bruised. His face was swollen, and he was wheezing. Songhiu returned in a while with another soldier identified as Yonga. The two lifted Bhugol and carried him back into the tent. They administered some first aid and gave him some water to drink. Bhugol was perplexed and wondered what had brought on this change of heart.

Moishan nodded at Songhiu. Songhiu began speaking.

'You look like a reasonable man. You understand the power and might of Lord Moishan. Your entire army ran into hiding within three days of battling us. How long do you think they can hide in their rat hole with a limited food supply? We have a deal for you. Give us what we want, and Lord Moishan promises that when he finally destroys this kingdom, he will not harm the elderly, children and women who cannot wield weapons.'

Bhugol remained silent.

'We have figured out that, based on the direction you were riding, your people must be hiding inside the fortress. How they entered it, we still don't know, because our men were on the lookout for nearly ten days after you all disappeared. Since we now know your hideout, we will attack and destroy everything there. We will burn the entire place to the ground. And you can watch it before you die.'

'What do you want from me?' Bhugol asked, finally relenting.

'Where are the prisoners from the two kingdoms? What

message did you deliver to the other kingdoms? What happened to Raakat and Khara?'

'I do not know where the freed prisoners are. They have been moved to some safe holding that has not been disclosed to any of us. I do not who Khara is? What I can tell you is that I delivered messages to the kings of Sangha and Anagraha, our allies in the first battle we fought against you. They have been informed to be at the battleground on the fifteenth day after the new moon of this month. Our king plans to wage a war as soon as they arrive. The battle plans and formations have not been divulged to low-ranking members of the kingdom like me.'

'Raakat was slain a few days ago when he tried to abduct two of our women from near the lake. These women are warriors, and they killed him. This is all I know. You may kill me if you like, but I do not know anything else,' said a broken Bhugol.

He believed that he had provided them irrelevant and half-baked information that would serve them no purpose. He had also mixed up the dates of arrival of the other armies, giving them a date that was two days later than the actual date. Additionally, he had also concealed the fact that he travelled to five kingdoms delivering messages, not just two. The poor man thought that this information may help save the elderly, the women and children if they ever came under attack. But if the barbarian was not going to keep his word, then it looked like they were all facing their death anyway. He reassured himself that he had done the right thing and that somehow, he had outsmarted them.

What came next was mind-numbing.

Songhiu said, 'Kidnap the grandchild of the king and bring him to us. We have no way to authenticate any of the information that you have just given us. Our only way to draw out your king out is by holding something dear to him as ransom. If you do not comply, we will storm that fort and bludgeon everyone to death. But we will first start will all the young ones, so that you can watch the future gems of your kingdom perish before your eyes. We will despoil every woman in there in front of her family and children. We will ruin everything that you hold dear and then, only then, will we kill your men. The choice is yours'

Bhugol collapsed to the floor, deeply anguished. He wished he had died before having to make this traumatic decision. The life of the innocent Prince Tanmay weighed against the lives and honour of all the women and children of Saptapuri! He had to make this heart-wrenching choice. Which option would be worse? Which would be considered the greater betrayal? As the debate raged in his head, he reasoned that perhaps sacrificing the life of one prince for the lives of the people of the kingdom was a small price to pay. Yet, he couldn't bring himself to come to terms with his choice. Prince Tanmay was just as precious as all the children of the kingdom—sacred and beautiful.

What if he agreed to their plan and then ended his life once he returned, he wondered.

Songhiu squealed with pleasure, as if he had read Bhugol's mind. 'Don't think you can fool us. If you die and the child doesn't come, we attack. If you tell them the truth and we don't get the child, we attack. Either way, by tomorrow the child should be in our barracks, or else at dawn on the third day, we will raze that pitiful fort to the ground. Is that understood?'

Bhugol nodded. He prayed that if the gods he believed in were watching, no harm would come to the little child. If not, sacrificing one child for the kingdom would be a guilt that he would have to carry to his pyre.

Betrayal

The war council waited anxiously for Bhugol's return. He should have been back by now. Worry creased their faces as they ate that morning. The preordained day for battle was just around the corner, and they had no idea whether Bhugol had successfully delivered their message to all the kingdoms. If he hadn't, they were going into battle with only half the numbers they had in the previous battle, walking towards certain death and destruction.

The Maharaja contemplated the future course of action. Would it come down to him using the Ajna Chakra? Would he have to endure the agony of living forever since the stone conferred immortality on its wearer? Wasn't there a way to simply destroy the stone? He made up his mind that if they ever survived this war, he would have to find a way to destroy the Ajna Chakra, even if it meant breaking the jewel to bits.

Just as they were finishing breakfast, Bhugol stumbled in, his face swollen and his body bruised badly. Gurupadaka rushed and grabbed him. They took him to the medical facility and administered first aid.

'What happened, Bhugol? questioned a worried-looking Gurupadaka. 'Were you attacked?'

'I had an accident, sir,' Bhugol gulped nervously. He wished he were dead. He was about to unleash a whole pack of lies to build on the one he had just told.

'After meeting King Grehan in Anagraha, I set off on my journey home, riding through the hills. I would have arrived last evening, but I had an accident. On a narrow path in the hilly forest, the horse tripped, causing me to fall. I tumbled down a steep slope, hitting several rocks and boulders along the way, until a cluster of trees broke my fall. I couldn't move for a long time and was pretty sure that I had broken a few bones. I was too afraid to call for help. What if I attracted the wrong people? Then I passed out from the excruciating pain for what felt like several hours. When I came to my senses, it was completely dark. With great difficulty, I crawled and leaned against some rocks for the rest of the night. It was cold, and I was shivering to the bone. When morning came, with every ounce of willpower I could muster, I climbed up the slope. The pain was unbearable, but I had no choice but to bear it. Fortunately for me, the horse had not wandered far from where I had fallen, and I spotted him grazing nearby. I managed to mount it and rode back despite the intense pain.'

'We are so relieved to see you back alive. You have no idea what an important task you have just accomplished. Our small numbers could not have countered such a mighty enemy. Knowing that you have conveyed our message to all the kingdoms has given us a much-needed ray of hope,' said Pashupati, sounding grateful to the minister.

'If only man could die of guilt,' thought Bhugol. The Maharaja and all the members didn't deserve to be lied to. The pain he was going to cause this family tore through his mind like a sharp arrow piercing his heavy heart.

'I have delivered the message to all the five kingdoms, my

lord. Queen Tara has sent vermillion from the temple of their deity for King Krishnakanth. All the other kings and their troops will be at the outskirts of the city at the stipulated hour,' he said, speaking the truth for the first time that morning.

Bhugol was unable to look any of them in the eye. His mind was racing, wondering where Tanmay was. How was he going to shake off the entire royal party and leave the medicine room? How would he isolate the boy and get him out of the fort?

Shankar sensed that something was not right. He smiled at Bhugol, who closed his eyes, feigning tiredness. It was hard enough as it was without Shankar's prying eyes fixated on him. Sometimes Shankar gave people the feeling that he could read their minds or see through their lies. But all he simply did was let things unfold the way they were meant to play out.

'God can redeem us only when we have tried our best to redeem ourselves. There is no greater absolution than admitting the truth. But I urge you to follow your heart Bhugol,' said Shankar so quietly that only Bhugol could hear it.

It was nearing sunset when pandemonium broke out in the fort, disrupting its normal functioning. Gauri was working on her potions in her room before dusk took away the natural light, when the door to her quarters was thrown open unceremoniously. A soldier entered, looking unapologetic but nervous. He looked around the room and was about to leave, not having found what he was looking for, when Gauri asked the soldier what the problem was. She could also hear the commotion in the corridors and the hallway and was curious about what was happening.

'Prince Tanmay is not to be found,' the man said hurriedly.

Gauri swiftly put the potions back into a wooden chest and

pushed it under her cot. She ran to the common area, where she saw a dishevelled-looking Princess Indumathi sitting on the floor and crying copiously. Her eyes were puffed and her face looked swollen. The usually composed Maharani Gautami sat beside her, looking upset and flushed. None of the men were around except for King Krishnakanth. He looked helpless as well. Gauri approached him and asked what had happened. He started to walk away towards the corridor and motioned to her to follow.

'Prince Tanmay did not return from play this afternoon. Normally, every day he comes back in the late afternoon to nap with his mother and father. After resting, he has fruits and milk just before dusk. But today the boy never showed up. When the chambermaid asked other children about him, they said he was playing with them after lunch. When they all dispersed, they saw him walking right behind them. The entire fort has been turned upside down, but there is no sign of the boy.'

'Where is everyone else?' she inquired.

'Searching the fort,' he replied.

'And Shankar?' came the next question.

'I saw him heading to the medical facility just a while ago."

Gauri thanked Krishnakanth and hurried to the medical facility. She found Shankar bent over a cot, examining the blood-stained sheets on it. He sensed her presence and turned around. Her enquiring look was sufficient, and she didn't have to ask him anything.

'Bhugol seems to have made a trade. Was it for his life or our lives, I don't know. But the child is in grave danger, and we need to find him as soon as possible. Do not breathe a word of this to anyone else. Find Manikanta and Anandamayi. We are going to go after Bhugol and the child.'

'Meet me outside the left-wing entrance with both of them. I will arrange for horses,' he added.

Gauri didn't need to be told twice. She found Manikanta first, as she was crossing the kitchen. He looked worried and didn't notice her. As he passed by Gauri, she caught him by his right arm, making him stop. She put a finger to her lips, indicating that he should remain silent. She then motioned for him to follow her quietly. Manikanta looked confused as he was in the middle of looking for the missing prince, but his immense respect and reverence for Gauri made him follow her. She continued walking, peeping into every room that they passed. With Manikanta in tow and looking utterly bewildered, she descended the steps leading led to the dungeons. She turned left at the end of the corridor when she saw Anandamayi walking towards them from the other end.

She rushed up to Anandamayi, pulled Manikanta closer and whispered, 'Please fetch your weapons and proceed to the exit leading out of the west wing of the fortress as soon as possible. Shankar will explain to you both what needs to be done. Do not speak to anyone else and let nobody know that you are stepping out of the fortress.'

Both Anandamayi and Manikanta had blind faith in Shankar. They didn't say a word and left immediately to get their weapons. Gauri herself went to fetch the sword that Shankar had given her during their last rescue operation. She found it, tucked it within the folds of her saree and ran up to the west-wing exit. When she reached up there, she found Shankar waiting with four horses. He smiled at her. Manikanta joined a few moments later. The three of them waited in silence for Anandamayi.

'I wonder what is keeping her,' Shankar wondered.

'I am here,' said a voice, as Anandamayi came around, carrying more weapons than she could single-handedly manage. She handed a small pipe and a quiver of poison darts to Gauri and gave her a small dagger. She then handed a shield to Manikanta and a dagger to Shankar. She strapped a shield to her back. Shankar nodded in approval. Gauri tucked the dagger and the poison darts into either side of her waist belt. She mounted the horse as did the rest of the party.

'Ride silently for some distance. When we are a little farther away from the fortress, we may speak freely,' requested Shankar.

The four of them rode on for a few miles until the fortress was a distant speck behind them. At that point, Shankar, who was riding ahead, motioned for them to stop. The other three slowed their horses down and jumped off, joining Shankar who was now standing at the edge of a row of trees under the setting sun.

'We need to save two lives,' announced Shankar. 'Bhugol seems to have been blackmailed and deceived into kidnapping our prince Tanmay.'

'How do you know this, Shankar?' interrupted Anandamayi.

'I sensed fear in his eyes this morning when I met him in the treatment room. He too has disappeared. But no one has noticed his absence because everyone's attention is solely focused on the little prince. Vidhushi mentioned that there were inconsistencies between what Bhugol shared and the pattern of his wounds and blood clots. His blood was clotted as if he had oozed blood for a while before it dried. A fall from the horse may cause cuts, scratches, bruises and bleeding, but his wounds were unlike that. He was tortured and beaten heavily, which led to bleeding.'

'The scoundrel!' swore Anandamayi.

Shankar shook his head in disapproval.

'Why should we save him? Nothing would ever make you kidnap a child, would it, Shankar? He should have just killed himself rather than committing this heinous act,' she spat.

'The facts are never that easy to comprehend, Anandi,' he said genially.

'I wish we all had your ability to look at people without judging them, Shankar! But we are ordinary people. I do not see why we should spend our energies in saving Bhugol. The boy is the only one who should be rescued,' she countered.

Shankar chose not to continue the conversation and just gave her his usual, reassuring smile.

'Bhugol would have reached his destination by now. From what our spies last conveyed, Moishan's army is camped on the outskirts of Amara. We must use the darkness to our advantage and stake out the area to see if we can discern their plan. Whatever they decide to do, they will make their move only in the morning. We must hurry,' said Shankar, sounding grave.

Bhugol stopped at the periphery of Moishan's camp. He looked at the innocent child, who was passed out on his horse.

Bhugol had snuck out of the infirmary after lunch when he knew that most of the people were either resting or were in their respective chambers. Only the children played outside in the safe area between the fourth wall and the moat. Tanmay was usually supervised by a chaperone. Bhugol had waited until the children had finished playing and began walking back in a single file towards the main living area. He was in luck, as the prince dropped his play stick and bent to pick it up, allowing all the other children to go ahead of him. The maid, who had no reason to suspect foul play, walked ahead, leading the children inside as she always did. Seizing this opportunity, Bhugol placed a scented cloth on Tanmay's nose from behind, causing the boy to swoon and lose consciousness completely. In a matter of a few minutes, he had the child on a horse and was riding towards their doom.

Bhugol feared handing Tanmay over to the devil himself. 'Was he doing the right thing?' he asked himself again. Was there a right thing in such a situation? He had to save tens of thousands of people, and if his life and the child's life were the price to pay, so be it, he thought. After all, Moishan had rightly figured out where the people of the kingdom were hiding. Moishan was also right in guessing that if he stormed the fort right away, the depleted and weakened Saptapuri forces wouldn't be able to fight back his strong army, leading to complete annihilation and massacre.

What Bhugol didn't understand then was Moishan's intention in asking for the child to be brought to him. It didn't make sense at all. Did he want to draw the people out to a fight before finishing them? In any case, he held the power to snuff out their entire kingdom if he wanted to. What was his intention then?

A goddess awakens

Moishan was pacing around his tent, balling his fists as he walked. The king's grandchild should have been here by now. It was nearing dusk, and the time that had been allotted to the foolish messenger was almost up. Had the man called his bluff? Had he told the royals about being caught and alerted them to the fact that their location was compromised?

'Bah,' he thought. If so, I will just storm their ridiculous fort and bring them to their knees. But that was not his plan. He didn't want to have a second battle with these idiots for one simple reason.

Moishan had asked for the child with a singular intention. He wanted complete leverage over the ruler of Saptapuri. Moishan had realized that he could wait for the spineless creatures to perish from hunger before finishing them off. However, in doing so, he ran the risk that if pushed over the edge, whether in battle or whilst hiding, the king might use the power of the stone for himself. If that happened, his dream of twelve long years would be crushed. He couldn't let that happen. He needed the sacred stone and its powers for himself. Once he had the power of the stone, he would destroy them all anyway.

Just as Moishan thought that the messenger would not return, Songhiu and Yonga brought Bhugol, who was carrying a young, sleeping child in his arms. It was a boy. Moishan grinned a most wicked, sickening grin. The Prince of Saptapuri, second in line to the throne, was a worthy leverage!

Bhugol stood in front of the monstrous chief, his eyes devoid of any hope. Moishan and his warriors began conversing in their brutish tongue and after some discussion, Yonga went out and came back with three more huge troll-like warriors.

Moishan had sent for his brothers because his plan now called for pure muscle power combined with stealth and speed. He had Simrik and Yonga for their stealth and speed; he had Songhiu, who knew the enemy tongue; and his brothers, unparalleled in using brute force. Moishan then proceeded to explain to them what exactly needed to be done.

He wanted the messenger and the child to be taken to the forest, a few miles away from the base camp. There, the brothers were to guard the child along with Yonga and Simrik, while Songhiu was to take the messenger back to the fort with a message for Maharaja Pashupati from Moishan.

Hand over the Ajna chakra by sunset or collect the head of your grandson, which will be speared to a tree outside your fort before the day ends.

The reason he wanted the child moved to the forest was that there was better cover, and if the king attacked them with a large force, Moishan's men would have the upper hand in a densely forested area.

Moishan also did not want anybody near his base camp before he was ready to launch an attack. He told the five men that under no circumstances should their focus shift from the child and that they should proceed to the forest at once. Songhiu was given instructions that after the party had found a suitable place to hide with the boy, he was to take the messenger to the king. He was to convey the message, including the location where they needed to bring the Ajna chakra and then head back with the messenger in tow. When the Saptapuri crew came to deliver the Ajna chakra, they were to be led to the base camp, with the child still held captive.

The party of five left with their weapons and prisoners. They decided to keep the boy sedated, while they tied and gagged Bhugol. Simrik tried to take charge as he felt undermined by Songhiu's talent for languages. He wanted to assert his authority but was sternly rebuked by Nishan: 'Don't forget your place when we brothers are here, or you will find your head rolling like Raakat's.' Both brothers then began to guffaw loudly. Suddenly, it dawned on them that they were on a discreet mission, so they toned down their laughter and continued taking digs at the low-ranking soldiers in whispers.

~

Manikanta and Gauri lay waiting in the low-lying grass, away from the wide ring road that led out of Amara. Their horses were secured in a stable some distance away. They were so still that they could have been mistaken for rocks. The night was as dark as the kohl lining Gauri's eyes, and their eyes strained to catch even the slightest movement around them. Though they expected nothing to happen in the dead of night, they were still on high alert.

Shankar and Anandamayi had gone towards the camp to see if they could spot anything. The little child would probably be traumatized and very scared. The two silently scouted the outer periphery of Moishan's camp, unsure of what they would learn or find. Even if they overheard someone talking, they did not understand the language to figure out what was being said. Still, they hoped to catch a glimpse of Bhugol or Tanmay.

Now that they had the child, Shankar feared that they might harm Bhugol. His intuition was correct. Right on cue, a group of hooligans walked out of one of the larger tents, with a sedated Tanmay in their arms, while a bleeding Bhugol, tied and gagged, was being forced to mount a horse.

They counted five gigantic men as they mounted their horses—two of them carrying torches, one the child, and two large men chuckling together.

Shankar and Anandamayi became super alert and tense. They signalled to each other in the pitch dark that they should alert Gauri and Manikanta. Slowly they crawled away from the encampment and made their way to where they had left Gauri and Manikanta. It was hard finding the two in the blackness of the night. Anandamayi was afraid that they would lose sight of the men in trying to find Manikanta and Gauri. But her fears were misplaced. The torches the enemies carried blazed in the dark, showing exactly where they were even from a safe distance.

They found Gauri and Manikanta, both of whom had also spotted the enemy's movement. Gauri had keenly begun to follow the movement of the enemy from where she lay, while Manikanta was vigilant about keeping them safe. Shankar and Anandamayi joined the two, and together they continued to wait in silence until they were sure that their enemy was nowhere within earshot.

They discussed their moves in whispers and signs. They decided that it was a good thing the prisoners were being moved away from the camp, even though they didn't understand the reason behind it. This way, they had fewer adversaries to deal with. They decided that following on horseback was dangerous because the sound of hoofbeats could alert the foe. The fire from the torches gave the enemy's position away in the dark, and the four warriors decided to use this to their advantage. They crawled and tiptoed away from the camp, staying in the shadows of the grass. Moving from tree to tree, they dropped down near bushes, crawling and hiding from sight as they followed the light of the torches from a safe distance. They followed Moishan's men through the night.

A light breeze had begun to blow, making the flames of the torches leap and flicker. However, Simrik and Yonga handled the torches deftly, so the breeze did not put them out. There was no sound to be heard except the rhythmic clip-clop of the hoofbeats. The five thug-like men were oblivious to the fact that they were being followed. It never once occurred to them to stop and look around to see if anything seemed amiss.

Shankar walked ahead, followed by Anandamayi and Gauri, with Manikanta bringing up the rear. The leaves had started rustling ever so slightly and the insects of the night were buzzing and chirping away, adding an eerie edge to the silence. They continued walking into the night, never once speaking to one another and continually watching out for the leaps and flashes of light from the barbarians' torches.

The problem arose as dawn approached. The enemy had reached the edge of the forest that stretched beyond. As the eyes began to adjust to the first blush of light, the prisoners and their captors entered the forests. All roads, built by the architects of Saptapuri, ended a few miles outside their town limits, converging with forests bordering their town. Now the trees were lending cover to the barbarians by masking the light from their torches. The flames danced in and out of sight as Moishan's men ventured further into the thick jungle.

Songhiu had kept the child sedated throughout their journey.

Yonga and Simrik, who were carrying torches to illuminate the path, turned to the Moishan's brothers and asked if they should extinguish the torches as the sky was beginning to brighten with the soft rays of the morning sun. The brothers nodded and the torches were put out.

The Saptapuri warriors, who were following at a distance, panicked as the flames suddenly vanished from sight. Without the guiding light of the torches, they would lose track of their enemies.

'Quicken your pace but be very vigilant,' said Shankar.

The four of them began moving swiftly towards the forest. As they were about to enter the forest, Shankar instructed them to be careful: 'Move stealthily, hiding behind the trees and boulders as required. Spread out a little bit so that we have eyes everywhere.'

Meanwhile, Moishan's men, with their prisoners had reached a small clearing in the forest. It was surrounded by tall trees and a few rocks were scattered here and there.

Shumran said, 'Let us halt. We can camp here while Songhiu takes the messenger and delivers our demands to the king of Saptapuri.'

'Simrik, you recce the area and check for any potential dangers,' ordered Shumran. Simrik nodded. He scowled at the misfortune of being stuck with the oafish brothers when he could have used this opportunity to impress Moishan. He picked up his weapons and walked away.

The child had started to rouse from his sedation, and Songhiu was about to place a scented cloth on his face once more when Nishan stopped him.

'Let the boy awaken. Let him feel the fear. Let it course through his veins like the blackest poison. He needs to look terrified when his people come to get him. His condition should instil such fear in their hearts that they are unable to raise a weapon in defence.'

Tanmay awoke from his deep sleep. His head was throbbing with pain. He felt groggy and his eyes took a long time to adjust to his surroundings. When they finally did, he was petrified to see that he was surrounded by enormous, fair creatures who looked like the monsters his grandmother had told him about in her stories. He was in the middle of a forest amongst these abnormal looking creatures. He was stricken with intense fear and started screaming for help.

Immediately, a hard blow landed on his face. Tanmay abruptly stopped howling. Blood rushed to his cheeks, and his whole face felt hot. A searing pain shot through his head. His fear turned to shock, and his howling became an indistinct whimper. Tears rolled down his face as he lifted his hands to protect it in anticipation of another blow. He fell to his knees and wrapped his arms around himself, shivering in fear.

It was then that Tanmay heard muffled sounds and saw another person trying to pull free from his restraints. It was an old, familiar face from his grandfather's court. The man had his arms bound behind his back, and his mouth had been stuffed with cloth to prevent him from screaming. The little child felt confused; he didn't know whether to be relieved that he wasn't alone or terrified by the minister's condition. The minister crawled towards him and shook his head, trying to communicate something with his tear-filled eyes.

Songhiu came close to the child and said harshly, 'Do not bother screaming and shouting. We are far away from your family. If you create a ruckus, we will hurt you.'

He then removed the gag from Bhugol's mouth and ordered

him to help the child understand the situation and keep him calm. Bhugol wanted, with all his heart, to wrap his arms around the child and comfort him. But all he could do was lie there and tell the child to be quiet.

'If you listen to them, they will not hurt you, my child. Please don't get hurt,' he pleaded, the pain writ across his face as his eyes brimmed with tears again.

Tanmay soothed his left cheek, which was stinging from the slap, with his cool palm. It had turned red as blood had clotted on his small face, and the imprint of his assailant's hand was clearly visible.

Pointing a finger at Bhugol, Shumran barked at Songhiu, 'You will leave with this filthy scum once Simrik returns from his reconnaissance.' Songhiu nodded in agreement.

A few miles away, Shankar and his team were getting desperate. They had lost track of the barbarians. They had been in the woods since dawn and the sun had risen high now, shining a brilliant orange on the eastern side of the jungle. Manikanta worriedly said, 'Have we truly lost them?'

'I hope not,' answered Anandamayi tersely. Life was throwing all kinds of curve balls at them. A kingdom whose peace had never ever been threatened was now on the verge of annihilation. For the first time, Anandamayi wanted to believe in the prophecy of the wise men.

'Oh, Shakti Ma! If you are truly meant to appear, do it now! We have never been more desperate and helpless, despite our strength and might,' she prayed fervently to the goddess of power.

The four of them continued to blend in with the trees, moving stealthily like shadows. After what seemed like an eternity, they thought they heard human voices. All four of them stopped in their tracks. Shankar was ahead of the others, his body pressed against a thick tree. Anandamayi was about four feet away to his right, also leaning against a tree. To Shankar's left, just two feet away, was Manikanta, stooping down at the base of a tree where clumps of roots entwined. Gauri was crouched next to a boulder behind all three of them, at a distance of four to five feet.

As she crouched behind the boulder, she checked whether all her weapons were in place. A sword in its hilt, a small dagger tucked into her the left side of waist belt and a small wooden pipe with poison-tipped darts to the right. She barely dared to breathe for fear of being detected.

The thickset trees of the forest grew so close to one another that they barely left room on the forest floor to walk. The roots had formed clumps the size of small boulders at the base of the trees. High above, the treetops merged into one another, creating a dark canopy that almost blocked the sun out. The sun's rays scattered through tiny gaps that they found between the thick overgrowth. Tiny circles of sunlight danced on the forest floor, illuminating a clearing ahead of them. Gauri peeped ever so slightly from behind the boulder to check for movement. All was quiet. Just when she was convinced that there was no immediate threat and that she could move, she heard the faintest breath behind her.

She leapt into the air, swung around swiftly while simultaneously pulling the dagger from her waist belt. As she landed on her feet, she slashed the man's throat in one neat line. Simrik dropped to his knees with a gurgling sound. The sand drank his blood, turning the ground red. The other three, who were close by, came running to Gauri's aid.

Just as Simrik fell, he threw something to the ground

near where the four Saptapuri warriors stood. The place was quickly enveloped in fumes. Gauri, possessing the instincts of an expert who had worked with chemicals, immediately held her breath. The other three, caught unaware, were paralyzed instantly. They could see and hear but were immobilized as their muscles stiffened. They kneeled over where they stood, looking towards Gauri helplessly.

Gauri knew that they had lost their element of surprise. She burst into the clearing ahead and saw four of the barbarians with Bhugol and Tanmay. The commotion had alerted them. Yonga and Songhiu held the terrified child between them, while Bhugol lay bound on the ground near their feet. Shumran and Nishan looked anxious, as their brother's perfect plan seemed to be coming apart.

Seeing Gauri, Shumran bellowed, 'She is just a stupid, puny woman. Crush her like a fly and get on with your task.'

Bhugol looked at Gauri with imploring eyes and said, 'Ma, please save the child. I have no excuse for what I have done. But please understand that it was for the good of our entire kingdom.'

Nishan moved towards Bhugol and kicked him hard in the chest. He cursed and said to Gauri, 'You wretched woman, leave now if you do not want to die. Your companions will also meet an ugly end if you interfere in our work.'

Gauri surveyed the place as he spoke. There were four of them against her. They also held the child, and she didn't want any harm to come to him. Behind her, on the forest floor, lay motionless the three real warriors who should have been fighting by her side. She didn't even have time to worry if they were okay.

Songhiu held a sword to Tanmay's throat and threatened Gauri, 'You make one move, and I will make sure you take the boy's head back to the fort as a decoration.' While he was screaming, his hand moved slightly and the edge of the sword nicked the neck of the child, causing him to shriek in pain. All four soldiers broke into an evil grin.

Seeing the blood on the child's neck, Gauri let out a loud, shrill scream that reverberated through the jungle. It was such a high-pitched sound that everybody dropped their weapons to cover their ears. The entire fauna of the jungle reacted to her shriek—birds took flight in large numbers, monkeys emitted distress signals and a flurry of other animals hurriedly fled the scene. As she stood there screaming uncontrollably, her body began emanating a kind of white light, as if her inner energies were externalizing and forming an aura around her. Tanmay who had also covered his ears, found an opportunity to run to the other side, taking cover behind Gauri.

Gauri stopped shrieking and drew her sword. Like a wild lioness, she went on a rampage. With her hair flying behind her and her eyes shining with fury, she flew at Yonga with her sword, chopping off his arm. He howled in pain and anger. The other three men grabbed their weapons from the ground and attacked her from all sides. Gauri swirled like a mighty tornado and kicked the three beasts, each of whom landed a few feet away. The fury on their faces knew no bounds.

A mere woman was giving the three warriors hell. She fought like a tigress, fiercely defending herself against the three massive, bear-like men. Each one came back at Gauri with full force, attacking repeatedly with their giant swords. They didn't give her a second to catch her breath, and thick jagged blades kept flying at her. She ducked and jumped around, skilfully moving herself out of the circle they had formed around her. Gauri now pulled out the dagger from her waist, brandishing a weapon in each hand now. She evaded a blow to the back of her head from the one-armed man, who had now gotten up and decided to join the fight. As he staggered off balance from his misaimed blow, she doubled back and shoved her dagger into the centre of his throat, twisting it in. She kicked his body out of her way. As she swung around, the man called Songhiu shouted in a menacing voice, 'The mighty brothers of Moishan shall not be defeated by a mere woman.'

His threat sounded more like a fearful show of bravado and a way to try and distract the warrior goddess.

'No woman is just a mere woman,' she spat at him. She leapt high up into the air, somersaulting in between the two heavy-set brothers, Shumran and Nishan. Their eyes widened in fear and disbelief, as they looked up at Gauri, nimbly making a landing between them, never realizing this was the last thing they would ever see. As she landed, she used the weapon in each hand to cut off both their heads simultaneously. As their bodies hit the ground and their heads rolled, Songhiu pulled up Bhugol and pointed the sword at his chest.

'Stop now,' in a hoarse, rasping voice.

Gauri looked at him. Her face was a storm of emotions, exploding with the ethereal radiance. She shook her head like a crazy lunatic, as if she hadn't heard a word of what he had said. She came running at him, her sword held high above her head. She was smiling—a haunting, sinister and ominous smile.

In a panic, Songhiu drove his sword into Bhugol, missing the chest and instead plunging it below the waist. Bhugol fell to his knees. With a roar, Gauri jumped up into the air, bringing down her sword forcefully on Songhiu's head. She drove it down hard, splitting his body down the middle.

She turned to Bhugol, consumed with rage. She wanted to

kill everything that moved and couldn't stop herself. Blinded by anger, she lifted her leg to kick him. As she was about to bring it down, someone clutched her hand. She furiously turned around to attack, but saw that it was Shankar. Seeing him, she went still, and her trance broke. She felt faint and dropped her weapons to the ground. The radiating aura around her receded, leaving her pale-looking and tired. She sank to the floor, only to be caught by Shankar's steady arms. He lifted and placed her on his lap.

Anandamayi and Manikanta had also recovered from the paralyzing effect of the fumes and rushed towards them.

Anandamayi enveloped a scared and shivering Tanmay in her arms to console him. She gently held the child's hand and walked him towards Shankar, who sat with a pale and almost lifeless Gauri on his lap. She touched Gauri's feet and said, 'Forgive me, Gauri! I had been blinded by my pride and envy.' Gauri was completely disoriented and unable to grasp what was happening around her.

Manikanta glanced at Shankar, who gestured towards Bhugol. Manikanta walked to a hurt and bleeding Bhugol and cut the ropes that bound him. He tried to pull the sword out of him, but the pain was excruciating and Bhugol pleaded to just let him bleed to death.

'I have wronged the child and the kingdom gravely. I do not deserve to live. I will not be able to carry this guilt through my life. Let it end here,' he begged. Manikanta ignored the request and sharply tugged at the sword, which was lodged deep in his flesh below the waist. Bhugol writhed in agony as the blade left him, and blood started gushing out of the wound. He looked at Manikanta with pleading eyes to put an end to his misery. But Manikanta was intent on saving his life. He tore his dhoti to bandage Bhugol's open wound to slow down the bleeding. Then he lifted the old man and helped him recline against a clump of roots at the base of a tree.

'Shankar, please leave me here to die, I do not dare to face the Maharaja or his family,' Bhugol addressed the senapati directly. Shankar looked at Manikanta and beckoned him. Manikanta walked over to the serene-looking army chief.

'Take Anandi and bring the horses. Make haste, for we do not want to be discovered with five dead bodies and people who cannot put up a fight right now. You cannot take Tanmay, as the child will only slow you down. Gauri and Bhugol are in no position to move at the moment. Hopefully, when you are back, Gauri will have come out of her stupor.'

∞

Manikanta and Anandamayi made a hasty retreat. The two tore through the jungle, covering ground in leaps and bounds, not slowing down to even catch their breath. In a few hours, they arrived at the stables of Amara with the sun still in the east. They quickly saddled the horses and made sure the two extra horses they were taking back to the forest were securely hitched together for safety. Silently, they led the horses onto the outer ring road, far away from Moishan's camp, and then mounted them. They rode in a parallel formation, with Manikanta and Anandamayi on the outer flank and the two extra horses in between.

All four horses were goaded to ride at top speed, keeping pace with each other and staying in formation, much like a chariot in battle. As planned, the two warriors reached the forest just around midday. They galloped into the clearing and found Gauri standing, covered in flecks of blood and looking resplendent, radiating a brilliant golden aura similar to a thousand suns.

A reckoning

Gauri stirred slowly and tried opening her eyes. But she was blinded by the sunlight. Her vision was blurry, and she blinked several times, rubbing her eyes furiously. She felt utterly exhausted as if she had run a full marathon. Slowly, memories began to surface. She remembered killing a fair, overgrown man in the woods and then running into a group of barbarians who had taken Tanmay captive. She also had a faint, albeit confused, recollection of fighting an entire bunch of brutes. Gauri wondered how she had acquired the superhuman strength to single-handedly kill five men and felt deeply mortified by the recollection of the savagery she had displayed in the forest. Was the whole thing even real? Or was she dreaming again?

Suddenly, she sat up with a jolt, like she had been hit by a hundred volts of power. Her dream had played out in reality. And its reality was more terrifyingly glorious than what she had ever experienced before. Her dreams had never been just dreams! They had been premonitions—a clear vision of what was destined to happen to her.

Though her heart felt heavy, Gauri did not feel an iota of remorse for what she had done. And in that moment, she realized that she was meant to deliver this land from evil. She was Durga, another manifestation of Goddess Parvati, who had assured her devotees that she would make an appearance to protect them from evil when the time came. In Saptapuri, she had chosen to appear as Mahagauri to triumph over demons and restore cosmic order.

Tears started flowing down her face as she came to terms with her reality. The moment she did that, she began exuding an aura that was almost golden and brilliantly luminous.

She became aware that she had been lying in Shankar's lap all this while. But she didn't try to move. She looked up at his divine face, tears continuing to stream down her cheeks.

Shankar smiled at her and pulled her close.

'I see the fear and confusion in your eyes, but I also see your powerful aura. You are conflicted, Gauri. I urge you not to be. The mother of all earth should have no confusion about herself and her purpose.'

'At a conscious level, we have limited powers because our energies are numbed by being trapped in a human body. That is a constraint. At a much deeper, meditative and unconscious level, we are eternally connected to the cosmos. There is oneness and abundant potential at this level. But in our normal waking state of consciousness, we are largely unaware of this immense potential and our connection to the collective because we are busy with the mundane. In deeper states of consciousness—such as dreams, deep sleep and meditation—we can connect more fully to this unlimited power. This is why your dreams have been trying to push your boundaries, and meditation has released your energies and bottled-up aura.'

'If you are familiar with the sacred verses of *Devi Mahatmyam*, you will recollect that the Goddess has two forms—one gentle and one terrible. Again Kaushiki (another manifestation of Goddess Parvati), is a projection of Parvati's *shakti* [power] to combat evil, though not conscious. You too are projecting your shakti now, Gauri.'

'And if it is of any comfort to you, Shiva, too, took the fierce forms of Bhairava and Veerabhadra, apart from his benevolent form as Shambho! This twofold complementary nature of your divinity—as both the auspicious and the terrible—is an ode to the play of light and dark. Both are aspects of your supreme being.'

Shankar smiled again. He wiped Gauri's tears and loosened his embrace, letting her stand up. She smiled back. In that very moment, she looked resplendent, radiating the magnificence of a thousand rising suns.

'I never told you about my dreams, Shankar!' Gauri whispered in complete bliss.

~

Bhugol had passed out due to weakness and exhaustion. Before Gauri had regained consciousness, Bhugol had pleaded with Shankar to take his life and spare him the guilt and shame.

'I will never see another peaceful sunrise in my life, oh noble warrior. Please let me go right now. Spare me the humiliation that goes with the guilt and the scars.'

'Bhugol, I understand what you tried to do. You believed with all your heart that the enemy had found us, and this was the only way to save many innocent lives. Your heart is in the right place. You are a good man who should never have to face humiliation or feel guilty for all that has happened,' Shankar said consolingly.

'Nobody knows how the prince disappeared. Everyone will be told that you came with me at my request to help save the prince. I assure you that you have not wronged the kingdom or the Maharaja. The child is safe, and we will not take one life to save one life.'

Manikanta carried the old man and gently placed him on his horse. He looked at the rest of the party and said, 'His body is cold. He needs medical attention immediately. We need to ride at lightning speed to take him to the rajvaidya.'

'Proceed Manikanta. We are right behind you,' said Shankar. 'Bhugol was injured badly while trying to help the prince. He left the palace with us, Manikanta,' Shankar said in a very matter-of-fact tone, conveying a clear message to his soldier.

'Of course, Senapati Shankar,' said Manikanta, quickly catching on.

Anandamayi quietly agreed to go along with Shankar's version of events. She seemed to have softened after seeing the almost lifeless old man. She helped little Tanmay up onto her horse.

Shankar and Gauri mounted their respective horses, and they rode as fast as they could towards the Adiparashakti fort.

Chaos all around

'Our men should return anytime now. Songhiu would have conveyed the message to the king, and I expect those bastards to come running with the sacred stone in their hands. Once we have it, we will slaughter them all,' said Moishan. Blood rushed to his head as he thought about how close he was to the stone and how he was going to wipe out the entire population of Saptapuri. He derived a perverse pleasure from thinking about all the blood and gore that lay ahead of him.

He ordered his men: 'Bring ten of the most brutal creatures in my squad. Let them prepare for the mass slaughter.'

A veil of sadness had descended on the Adiparashakti fort. The royal family had searched every nook and cranny of the fort for Prince Tanmay. They had walked along the boundary walls of the towering fort and also scoured the surroundings. Prince Chandrasekhara and a few men even risked stepping out and riding around the periphery of the fort, looking for the little prince. What was most perplexing was that Shankar was nowhere to be found. He was normally the most level-headed person during a crisis.

'Where the bloody hell is Shankar?' bellowed Pashupati.

Everybody in the hall looked at one another and shrugged their shoulders. Nobody could find Shankar. His absence infuriated Pashupati even more. It was frustrating enough that they had a missing child, and now they had a missing senapati too.

'How irresponsible of him to not be around when I need him the most,' thought the Maharaja. Pashupati was storming around the dining hall, looking both furious and helpless. All his ministers stood on the sidelines, watching him pace like a wounded animal.

Chandrasekhara returned from doing a perimeter sweep and went straight to his wife. He embraced her, and she looked at him with questioning eyes. He shook his head. His shoulders slumped; his face was grave and his eyes seemed hollow. He lowered his head onto Indumathi's shoulder to hide his tears. In the privacy of their chamber, the couple broke down—one without restraints and the other silently, feeling utterly defeated. Darkness had fallen, and the moon was waxing after the full moon of the previous week. There was nothing more to be done right now. The prince and his consort cried into the night, grieving the loss and trying to fight the pain in their hearts.

The Maharaja paced the dining hall all night. Even the Maharani had lost her usual composure and had let her grief get the better of her. She sat at the table with her head down, not once looking up. For the first time in history, the royal family were no longer men and women holding titles or administrative powers; they were simply parents and grandparents who had lost their child.

Earlier in the evening, the entire fortress had been combed thoroughly and a headcount had been taken to determine if anybody else was missing. This exercise had been carried out by Raja Krishnakanth at the suggestion of Acharya Veni to rule out the possibility of a kidnapping conspiracy.

'Desperate times called for desperate measures,' said the Acharya. He further added, 'Someone on the inside could have taken the boy to demand something from the Maharaja—such as handing over the Ajna chakra to the enemy in exchange for sparing the kingdom.'

At some point nearing dawn, Krishnakanth realized that it was not only Shankar who was unaccounted for but so also Anandamayi, Bhugol, Gauri and one of the younger soldiers, Manikanta. This seemed to give Krishnakanth a little hope. If Shankar, Gauri and Anandamayi were missing, along with Bhugol, then Shankar must have figured out something that he didn't want to share with everyone. Krishnakanth decided to keep it that way and didn't share his thoughts with anyone.

Inside their private chamber, Indumathi had gone from sobbing to reminiscing. She was held Tanmay's garments in her hands thinking about his favourite colour, which brought out the sparkle in his eyes. She cradled his favourite wooden toy, a small colourful elephant with its baby at its heels. She let her tears splash over the toy as she imagined the child playing with it. Meanwhile, Chandrasekhara thought about the first time he held his newborn son. It had been the best moment of his life, a moment of pure joy and happiness.

The two refused to eat a morsel of food. Gautami tried to get her son and her daughter-in-law to eat something; but it was an exercise in futility. Her coaxing only made them cry more. Even she didn't believe most of what she said to the two to comfort them. Her words sounded hollow to her own ears. So, she let them be.

Gautami headed back to the meeting room where the

ministers and the royals had regrouped after completing their morning routines. It had been a whole day since Tanmay went missing and Pashupati had lost all hope of finding him. Everyone who had helped with the search had reached the same conclusion, but no one dared to voice it.

'Where the bloody hell are my brothers?' screamed Moishan. His temper was out of control. He was raging that his brothers and their prisoners were not back with the scum from the Saptapuri kingdom.

Moishan wasn't the patient type. He had never waited long to get anything he wanted in life. He hit and took. He killed and took. But he took what he wanted, when he wanted. Waiting was not his style. But this stone had made him wait twelve long years. And now that he was so close to it, his impatience only grew. If only he had gone into the battle the first time, he could have plucked the king's eyes out, smashed his skull, taken the stone, and wiped out the population of the kingdom.

The setting sun had bathed the sky in a delicate golden hue. Hidden behind clouds, it looked like a jewel, a pendant of the gods. Pashupati was gazing out of the window when he suddenly heard a commotion and loud chatter. He turned around to see a bunch of people enter the meeting hall. Among them was a little child, worn and dirty, trying to wriggle out of Anandamayi's tight hold and run towards Gautami. It was his grandson, Tanmay!

At the door stood Shankar, Gauri and Manikanta. Beyond that, nothing else registered in Pashupati's eyes. He rushed to his grandson and enveloped him and Gautami in an embrace. Gautami held Tanmay tightly as she whimpered, tears rolling down her cheeks. The boy too was shivering uncontrollably and crying along with his grandmother. Within seconds, Indumathi came rushing into the hall and grabbed her son from the Maharani's embrace. News of his arrival had reached her through her chambermaids the moment Tanmay entered the first gate of the fort. She looked him up and down to see if he was all right and then she too embraced him tightly with tears in her eyes. Chandrasekhara stopped at the door and revelled in the sight of his wife cuddling their son. He couldn't believe their child was back with them. He walked slowly towards Indumathi and whispered to her, 'Take him back to the private chambers. He probably needs food and sleep.'

Indumathi nodded. She picked up the child and headed towards her chamber, beckoning the chambermaids for food and water.

The attention then shifted to the group standing at the door and the lifeless form that they had put down at their feet.

'He is no more, your majesty,' announced Manikanta. Pashupati walked towards the lifeless body of Bhugol lying on the floor. He looked at Shankar with questioning eyes.

'His body needs a quick yet dignified cremation, Your Majesty.' Then we need to rapidly put our plans into action. We don't have time anymore.'

They went about planning Bhugol's cremation. Gauri, Manikanta, Anandamayi and Shankar felt the pain of losing a good man. Even Anandamayi had come to realize that the old man had everybody's best interests at heart when he did what he did. His guilt seemed to have eaten through his will to live, and life slowly ebbed from him as they rode back to the fortress. Everyone said their prayers and bid their farewell to Bhugol. Gauri shed a tear for the man who would soon be celebrated as a hero in the days to come.

During dinner that evening, Anandamayi and Shankar took turns explaining what had transpired. Shankar wove a narrative that concealed Bhugol's involvement in Tanmay's kidnapping to ensure that the minister's reputation remained unsullied.

He said, 'None of us know how Tanmay left the fortress. But what we can say for sure is that when Bhugol fell from his horse and was unconscious for a while, he had been spotted by the enemy. He was followed back to the fortress, and the enemy had their eyes on us. Somehow, they got a hold of Tanmay. Whether they knew he was the prince or not, we are not sure. Bhugol approached me when we were searching for Tanmay and told me that he suspected that he had been followed and that Tanmay may have been kidnapped. I realized that we needed to take immediate action. Bhugol volunteered to come with us since he had a better knowledge of the forests from his recent travels. We found the child with a bunch of ruffians in the jungle, where they had him sedated. Two of the four men killed in the rescue operation were Moishan's brothers.

This was their ploy to force us to give up the Ajna Chakra. Very soon, Moishan and his men will discover that they have no leverage over us and that his brothers are dead. Once that happens, we will be attacked immediately.'

Anandamayi explained to her attentive audience how she, Shankar and Manikanta had been paralyzed and how Gauri transformed into a goddess, killing five men and rescuing Tanmay single-handedly. She also mentioned that while Bhugol didn't take part in the fight, he was taken hostage and was stabbed before Gauri could help him. Everyone looked at Gauri in utter awe while she sat at the table, blushing.

'This still leaves us vulnerable as Tanmay could not have left the fort on his own. We have a traitor amongst us. This is grave,' announced Gautami.

Chandrasekhara, who was relieved that his son was back, said, 'You are right, Mother. This is a grave situation. I will always be grateful to Bhugol's family for his sacrifice, but our immediate focus needs to be on the impending battle. If the traitor survives the war, we will have an inquiry later.'

'Shankar, you take enough men through the tunnel to the Pataleshwar fort so that you may ready the horses. Come to the battleground with cavalry and the elephants. Please tell Vidhushi and her medical assistants to set up camp at the perimeter of the battlefield.'

Gurupadaka said, 'The armies of all the kingdoms have arrived at the border, and we shall meet them at dawn with the battle plans. Our soldiers will join us on the battlefield the same evening. The day after tomorrow, we fight.'

'The Ajna Chakra, fully encased, will be carried at the centre of the Surya chakra, composed exclusively of the Kabali. Our cavalry, elephants and foot soldiers will provide protection from the front, while the archers and reserve soldiers will guard our rear,' added Anandamayi.

'Gauri, you will be a part of the cavalry, so go with Shankar and come back to the battlefield on horseback.' Then Anandamayi gave instructions to Manikanta, standing at the door. 'Go down to the weaponsmith. I had asked him to forge a special weapon a month ago, and it should be ready by now. Please fetch it from him right now.'

Shankar looked at Anandamayi with a quizzical expression. Ever since Gauri had killed Moishan's general Raakat, Anandamayi had been impressed and started to show more respect towards Gauri. But after seeing Guari's spectacular fighting skills that morning, Anandamayi had nothing but reverence for her.

Shankar was pleasantly surprised at what Manikanta brought back. He handed Anandamayi the most beautiful looking, sharp and majestic *trishul.* Anandamayi thanked him and took it.

She turned to Gauri and explained, 'This trishul has been forged especially for you, Gauri. The metal for it has been obtained from the temples of Brahma, Vishnu and Maheshwara. The weapons and accessories of Durga, Lakshmi, and Saraswathi too have been melted to create the final weapon. I pray that the fierceness of Bhairava and the roaring strength of Rudra, along with the vision, clarity and benevolence of all our gods, are channelled to you when you use this weapon.'

Everyone nodded in agreement. Shankar smiled at Anandamayi and said, 'Hara Hara Mahadev! May the lord destroy all our problems.' Gauri was speechless and quietly took the trishul from Anandamayi.

She thought about the strange turn her life had taken over the past couple of months. If her parents or friends knew that she was willingly going to war, they would lose their minds. She smiled as she thought of them. Ananya would have freaked out and made some stupid comments about her bravado. Suddenly, it hit her that her people were not here. She felt a jolt, as if a stone had dropped in her stomach. All the people in this room were going to say goodbye to their loved ones and step into battle. She, on the other hand, had nobody. She was an alien, going into battle for an alien cause, not knowing if she would come back alive or if she would ever make it back to her world.

Holding the trishul in her hand, Gauri closed her eyes and inhaled deeply, envisioning a triumphant victory for Saptapuri and her safe return home. In the moment, she looked ethereal, and everyone in the room could see it. She opened her eyes, expressed her gratitude to Anandamayi, her radiant glow having faded.

Ending darkness

Moishan had waited all evening. His hair stood on end as he imagined the energy and power of the Ajna Chakra. He had been told that the stone was forged from the fire of the 'third eye' of a deity that the locals worshipped. He laughed! No divinity they knew would possess as much power as he would once he got the stone.

'But enough of daydreaming,' he chided himself. Where were the five men? He was beginning to wonder if everything was alright. After all the scumbags of Saptapuri had thwarted him twice until now. The first time, by making all their people disappear even as the battle was still raging. The second time, by freeing his prisoners of war from the two conquered kingdoms and killing Raakat along with some of his other men. His prized general's head had come back to him in a bag! His blood boiled at the very thought. It wasn't that he missed Raakat; it was pure rage at having been humiliated. Moishan stamped his foot on the ground with such hatred that the earth shook. The two men standing guard at the entrance of his tent came running inside to see what had caused the tremor!

'Tell the men to be ready in the morning. We are going to go search for my brothers. The overfed oafs only have big bellies and no brains. I have to take care of everything.'

The search party set out early in the morning. Every soldier was trembling with fear. It was not often that Moishan himself headed a search party or a hunt. His love for violence was spoken of in fearful whispers in the barracks. Nobody wanted to get on the wrong side of their leader. Also, no one had a clue what could set him off. Every soldier headed out with trepidation, hoping not to be the reason for Moishan's temper to flare.

They rode along a long, winding path, galloping at a steady pace. The path was a beautiful one if one stopped and paid attention to it. It was a wide, muddy road bordered by fields dotted with yellow flowering shrubs, small trees and dew-covered grass. But this pack of men was akin to devils. They never stopped to breathe in the fresh air or admire nature. They had never been allowed to enjoy a sunset or watch children play. They just knew how to overrun anything bright and beautiful, leaving behind mass destruction, gore and tears.

The group soon entered the forest and followed a steep path that climbed up a small hill. Moishan thought that he might get a better view from the height, giving him a clearer perspective. It took them the better part of the day to reach the summit. When they reached the top, they stopped at a spot that offered a clear, unobstructed view of the surrounding landscape. It was late afternoon, and the sun was still bright. They were a couple of hours away from sunset. In the distance, miles away, they caught sight of the fort where the people of Saptapuri had holed up.

Moishan had developed many skills over the years of leading a nomadic life, including a keen sense of observation. From his vantage point atop the hill, he noticed an unusual flurry of activity amongst the wildlife on the forest floor below. Vultures and eagles were circling a spot to the left of where he stood.

The sound of howling and growling from various carnivorous animals echoed through the jungle, indicating they had found a sizeable prey to scavenge upon.

Moishan decided to check the spot out. He was just about descend the hill when something else caught his attention. He could discern some activity at the Saptapuri fort. From the dust rising, it was clear that their army was on the move. Moishan felt extremely disconcerted. He didn't like what he was seeing. What had caused their troops to get moving? They were supposed to be bringing him the Ajna Chakra, not gearing up for a battle!

'Damn,' he thought. He urgently needed to figure out where his brothers were. Chakra or no chakra, he had to find them soon and get back to base. It seemed like the people of Saptapuri wanted to go to war, and it amused him. He decided to investigate the commotion in the forest before heading back to base. Mounting his horse, he began riding speedily towards the forest.

A resounding cry tore through the forest floor when they reached the disturbed spot in the jungle. Moishan found the dead carcasses of his brothers and soldiers. He howled like a wounded animal, enough to scare away the birds circling above. However, the jackals trying to feast on the bodies lingered and growled at Moishan. They bared their teeth at the soldiers, as if daring them to come closer to the bodies.

Moishan jumped off his horse and lunged at the jackals. Having never known fear in his life, he brandished his weapon at the animals. One of the jackals jumped at him and caught his fist between its jaws, its teeth sinking deep into his flesh. Moishan twitched slightly but remained unfazed. He was a gargantuan man; he lifted his arm, with the jackal still clinging to tightly it, and swung the animal around until it was dizzy.

He then flung it with such force that its neck broke when it hit the ground. A painful howl echoed through the air as its life ebbed away.

Two more jackals attacked him simultaneously—one pouncing from the front and bowling him over, and the other grabbing his leg as he fell. Moishan writhed around a bit, trying to get a grip on the animals. He grabbed the jackal on his leg and tore it away, ripping some of his own skin in the process. The other jackal was standing on his chest now, its teeth inches away from Moishan's face. He grabbed it by its throat and, with the fury of a seasoned slayer, he dashed the heads of both jackals together. The howls of the animals were mixed with the sound of their skulls cracking on impact. Both animals dropped to the floor, dead. The rest of the jackals simply scurried away.

Moishan checked his wounds, tearing off a piece of his clothing and wrapped it around his leg. He then knelt between the headless bodies of his brothers and pulled them closer to him. He checked for identification marks on both bodies to ensure that it was his brothers.

'Pick up the heads and bodies of Shumran and Nishan,' Moishan said quietly to the soldiers. His voice was almost a whisper. The soldiers had never heard Moishan talk like that. Could their leader be feeling a new kind of emotion? Did he feel sad at the loss of his brothers? No one could tell, because a moment later, Moishan stood up and screamed at the top of his lungs, so that the entire forest echoed with his voice.

'War! War! War!' screamed Moishan. 'I will rip their hearts out of their bodies. I'll make sure that not a single man, woman or child has a limb left when I am done. This land has brought complete and utter destruction upon itself. I will not be defeated! Get the hell back to the camp and prepare for battle. We will wipe their race out! I am God, I am the Almighty! I am unstoppable! It is time to show them that.'

'Be careful as you tread. Watch your heads and arms, men,' Shankar called out. Gauri and Shankar led the procession of soldiers walking through the tunnel to Pataleshwar Fort. They had reached the alcove from Adiparashakti and were making their way towards the underground fort. Shankar crouched and crawled through first, extending his hand to Gauri, who followed suit. She smiled at him. Even when the going was tough, seeing Shankar's face always made Gauri smile. It seemed like an automated response. Shankar smiled back at her. 'Watch your head,' he repeated. Gauri crawled out and joined him as he opened the other door and crawled through on all fours once again. Gauri followed him. The soldiers reached Pataleshwar within three days, not stopping anywhere for rest.

Vidhushi seemed to have been expecting them. 'I have been expecting you,' she said.

The soldiers were given food and told to get some sleep before they headed out the next morning. Vidhushi assigned two of her best physicians to stay back at Pataleshwar to care for the soldiers who had yet not recovered from the earlier battle. Meanwhile, the rest began packing medical and surgical supplies to take to the camp, which they were supposed to set up near the battle site.

At the crack of dawn, the mighty cavalry, elephants and foot soldiers departed for the battlefield. The soldiers who had healed well joined their ranks too. At the helm, riding out with the soldiers, were Shankar and Gauri.

At the Adiparashakti fortress, only the women and children

were left behind as all able-bodied men, soldiers and the Kabali headed out to the battlefield. Each woman performed prayers and placed vermillion on the forehead of her man, wishing him luck and victory before they left. Gautami did the same and after applying vermillion on Pashupati's forehead, she pulled him into a tight embrace.

'Go be the man I chose to marry all those years ago. May valour, strength, kindness and compassion combine to lead you down the right path. May Saptapuri be victorious,' she said, as she let go of him reluctantly. Pashupati turned and walked away without a word, lest his brimming eyes give away his feelings.

Pashupati felt a deep sense of gratitude as he received the kings of all the neighbouring lands into his tent to discuss the battle plans. Gurupadaka and Chandrasekhara explained formations and war strategies to the kings and their generals in detail.

The Ajna Chakra which was at the heart of conflict, stood securely in its casing, surrounded by the fiercest warriors that the southern lands had seen. A soft purple glow radiated from the stone, resembling a halo. In the past few weeks, the stone's properties had changed. It had begun acting in a strange manner. There appeared to be an electric charge around the stone, and it had begun to spark and flicker. It seemed as if the it knew that there was going to be a change in its destiny soon. It was as if the stone were alive!

Pashupati stepped out of his tent in time to see the cavalry arrive. Riding at the front were two radiant figures, Gauri and Shankar. Pashupati smiled as he looked at them, thinking to himself what a lucky man he was. In the face of uncertainty and distress, he had these two on his side. It was as if Shiva and Shakti had descended upon the earth to deliver them from evil!

'Whatever happens, we are in good hands,' he thought to himself.

Even before the sun rose, all the kingdoms of the Oundin range had taken position on the battlefield as per instructions. At the forefront of the Garuda Vyuha, leading all armies, were Kings Pashupati, Krishnakanth, Grehan, and Prince Chandrasekhara on elephant backs. The left wing of the Garuda had Kings Girijapati and Siddheshwara. The right wing had Kings Prajapati and Samara. Behind them was Shankar and the cavalry. Gauri rode a beautiful grey and white horse, and she stood to the left of Shankar, who was pleased at having his horse Nandi back with him. The generals from all the other kingdoms were strategically placed across the wingspan of Garuda to lead the soldiers.

In the middle of the Garuda, enveloped by its large wing formation, was the Kabali. They were in the formidable Surya chakra formation, with foot soldiers holding shields and spears forming rays of the sun. At the centre was Anandamayi, on a horse, carrying the powerful Ajna Chakra. It had become strangely charged and was erratically sparking from time to time. The glow too had become stronger and more pronounced.

The rear end of the formation was completed by foot soldiers who formed the tail of Garuda. The flags of all the kingdoms fluttered in the wind as they were being held high by the foot soldiers. Everyone waited anxiously with pounding hearts for the sunrise, which will herald the start of the battle.

Facing the allied armies was a sea of humongous men clad in black, their pale, white skin contrasting starkly. Far at the back of their ranks, Moishan stood hoisted on a platform. Even with the distance between the two armies, the allied soldiers shuddered at the sight of the Buffalo Demon! He was everything that they had heard about and expected to see. Yet, seeing him in person only increased the trepidation they had felt all along.

The sun came up, and war cries rent the air along with the loud blast of the bugle and the beating of drums.

'*Hara Hara*!' cried Shankar. '*Hara, Hara*!' responded the charged soldiers. The war cry reverberated on the battleground.

Both armies rushed forward, crashing into each other's frontlines like waves upon the rocks. Moishan's soldiers outnumbered those of the allied armies three to one. They smashed and bludgeoned their way through the forces of Saptapuri and its allies. But the men would not relent. Their loyalty to their kings, their kingdom and everything they held sacred was on the line now. Every ounce of their courage had to be summoned as they faced Moishan's demons head on. An unholy chill had settled over the battleground, increasing the dread of what was to come.

The generals of Moishan's army were like large grizzly bears. Their single smack alone could finish off a soldier. Two generals, in particular Chonden the fierce and Meuden the bald, were spreading terror and mayhem on the battlefield, causing the allied forces to run helter-skelter.

Very soon, the sands of the field had soaked up enough berry-red blood to look like a carpet of death. Corpses lay dismembered throughout the grounds and the already outnumbered allied forces were dwindling rapidly. The kings and generals were having a tough time keeping the Garuda Vyuha intact. The Surya Chakra was nearly exposed when Shankar sounded a short blast from his conch shell, signalling that they needed to regroup.

They had barely regrouped with Shankar at the helm when Chonden and Meuden came crashing into their ranks, trampling soldiers beneath their heavy feet. They clubbed and slashed at the cavalrymen around them. Horses fell with neighing cries, their feet and flanks mutilated and clobbered by heavy weapons. Misty red sprays filled the air, and it seemed that the sky was turning red with all the bloodshed.

Gauri felt the darkness deep within her as she breathed in the smell of blood-soaked earth. She turned her horse around to see the two generals who had breached her ranks. She jumped off her horse and patted it. She whispered something into the animal's ears, and it tore away from the battlefield at lightning speed.

She then pulled out her weapons and stomped the ground with all her might. The earth cracked beneath her feet, and the fissure ran all the way to Chonden's feet. His eyes followed the crack to its origin and was surprised to see a woman on the battlefield. She looked glorious! She looked resplendent! She looked divine! And yet all his dull, numbed mind could think was how she would make a splendid addition to Moishan's bedroom! After all, any maiden who survived Moishan was theirs to feast upon later. He called out to Meuden above the clashing of swords and the blizzard of spears. He pointed towards Gauri. Most of the soldiers around the two generals became still. Shankar too was among them.

Suddenly the air was rent with fresh war cries.

'*Ambe Gauri*!' cried Manikanta. Instantly, all the generals and soldiers encircling Gauri started chanting '*Ambe Gauri! Ambe Gauri!*' over and over again.

Incensed by the war cries, Gauri became energized. The chant was replaced by the sound of beating drums and hymns in her head. Blood coursed through her body, making her look flushed. Her radiance lit up the entire field. It was as if someone had parted the clouds and let the sunshine upon everyone.

Gauri charged at the generals, rotating a weapon in each

hand. She was so quick and nimble as she changed between weapon and shield as she attacked that the two generals didn't last more than a few minutes.

Gauri blocked Chonden's sword with her shield and aimed a powerful blow at his chest with the hilt of her sword. Chonden's ribs cracked, and he dropped his sword, clutching his chest. She swiftly turned her blade at an angle and plunged it into his sternum, tearing through his heart. As she pulled out the blade, blood gushed forth with mighty force, bathing Gauri's white saree in bright red. It was all done in a flash even before Meuden could raise his weapon.

She then turned to face Meuden, who lifted his club high above his head, aiming for Gauri's. Gauri reached for her dagger and sent it flying at him. It hit him between the eyes. He staggered as he tried to pull the dagger out of his face. Still fuming and raging, she grabbed Meuden by his hair, dragged him and threw him onto Chonden's dead body. Then she drew her sword and pushed it through Meuden's torso, pinning him to the dead Chonden, binding them both to the ground.

By this time, the Buffalo Demon's army had penetrated the Garuda Vyuha and shattered the formation to bits. The Surya Chakra, which was now exposed, began defending its prized possession with ferocity. Each Kabali warrior was so strong that the heavyset soldiers of Moishan fell like dead birds from the sky. Reinvigorated by the protection granted by Mahagauri, the army renewed its efforts to defend their lines.

Moishan was an embodiment of all dark qualities of human nature—avarice, aggression, shallowness, jealousy, dishonesty and vengefulness. Drawn to the gleam of light across the battlefield, Moishan thundered through the field, slaying soldiers with his sword and trampling others under the wheels of his massive chariot. Three of his most formidable generals were beside him. Damron, Durdon and Dumukan shielded their lord as he steered closer to the centre of the allied army.

Moishan could feel the presence of the stone. They had brought it to him after all. As he was taking pleasure in clubbing each of his opponents to death, he came face to face with a tall, formidable-looking old man. He had a long white beard and wore a red dhoti and his body armour had the emblem of Saptapuri on it. The old man threw his spear at Moishan, who dodged it with ease. He, in turn, flung a weapon that had two spiked balls, joined by a chain.

The old man, Acharya Veni, dodged it. He brought his horse closer to Moishan's monstrous vehicle and pulled out his sword. But he didn't get very far. A heavy club landed on his back, splitting his spine into two. The Acharya fell to the ground, catching Gauri's beautiful eyes as his own closed forever.

Gauri's anger knew no bounds as she saw Acharya Veni fall to the ground. She wanted to put an end to the death and destruction that this Buffalo Demon was causing. But to get to him, she had to destroy his generals first.

Damron, Durdon and Dumukan spread like dark smoke around Moishan, making it hard for her to reach him. She noticed that the Kabali had also scattered due to Moishan's uniquely designed chariot. At the front of the chariot, there was an ominous-looking buffalo head with massive horns extending out on either side. To avoid being impaled by its horns, the soldiers jumped out its way, shattering their formations.

With all the havoc wreaked by the enemy force, only a thin line of soldiers remained between Anandamayi and Gauri. Anandamayi sounded three short blasts on her bugle, signalling that she needed backup. Shankar, Chandrasekhara, Samara,

Krishnakanth, Manikanta and Maharaja Pashupati rode up between Gauri and Anandamayi.

Kings Krishnakanth and Samara had been forced off their elephants by Moishan's army and were now on horseback. Maharaja Pashupati alone remained on his elephant. He looked down at the cold-blooded, evil face of Moishan, whose small black eyes looked back at him with a vengeance. They seemed to be asking Pashupati if this bloodshed was enough or if he wanted more. Pashupati then directed his sight towards Gauri, and Moishan looked in the same direction as well. He noticed for the first time the exquisite woman standing before him on the battlefield.

She was a jewel herself. More beautiful than any jewel or stone he owned. She glowed as if the sun had been infused into her skin. Her hair flowed like molten lava, and her lips looked redder than all the blood he had shed that day. But her eyes burned like flames—they sparkled and danced as she looked at him. He would have her, just as he would have the sacred stone! His brain and his loins were on fire simultaneously, and he looked to his generals and barked some orders. The generals charged at the line of defence that separated Moishan from the Ajna Chakra. They waged a ferocious attack on the Kabali soldiers. Shankar and Manikanta along with Prince Chandrasekhara and other princes, joined together to form a protective circle around Anandamayi. Gauri, seeing that Anandamayi was protected, went after Damron, the coward who had attacked Acharya Veni from behind!

As the fight raged on, a fierce, blustering wind started blowing suddenly. Dust was whipped into the faces of the soldiers, making it difficult for them to continue fighting. They could barely stand upright and most had abandoned their weapons to stay rooted to the ground.

Gauri seized a handful of arrows and took aim. Moishan silently laughed at her folly. The gusty winds would scatter her arrows like a buffalo flicking flies off its back with a swish of its tail. Gauri stood like a rock, unwavering even as the winds stormed around her. She pointed in the direction of the deceitful Damron and let six arrows fly in succession. The fletching on the arrows caught the wind and turned them slightly. Moishan's amusement turned into shock when two of the arrows whizzed past Damron and struck Durdon in the pit of his neck, severing his artery. He spluttered blood from his mouth, and his eyes froze in horror as the realization dawned that his end had come.

The four remaining arrows seemed to be carried by the howling wind straight to their target. They pierced Damron's body and he fell to the ground, joining multitudes of bodies and the scattered entrails of comrades and enemies alike.

As suddenly as the gusty winds had begun, they stopped. Gauri, who had not flinched during the storm, hastened towards the remaining general. She reached him in a matter of seconds, roaring into his face to catch his attention. Dumukan turned white as if he had seen an apparition. Gauri was blazing as if she were on fire. She embraced Dumukan, squeezing him so hard that his ribs cracked, causing him to collapse like a pile of bones!

Moishan, having watched his most powerful generals being decimated, was in a frenzy. His head was spinning. All his hatred and fury had come to the fore now. What witchcraft was this ethereal beauty dabbling in? How did she manage to kill his most powerful generals? Fear had finally caught up with Moishan. He needed the stone now so that he could become immortal, and then crush this woman under his feet. He thundered towards Anandamayi, brandishing his sword and whip.

All the kings, princes, and soldiers tried stopping Moishan, one by one, but in vain. Moishan rent the air with a bellow that tore through the ears of all on the field. He ripped apart every single man who tried to stop him, leaving behind a trail of mutilated and bloodied bodies, half alive, in his wake.

Gauri now leapt into his path, giving vent to the full fury of her wrath. She shone as bright as the sun above as she lashed out at Moishan with a spear. She grabbed his own whip, noosed it around his head and began pulling it tight. But the beast shook it off and charged at her. She struck him with her sword, but it seemed to bounce off his thick skin. Fuelled by a rage paralleling Moishan's, Gauri then tried to rain arrows upon him. He shielded himself and jumped away from her, trying to get to Anandamayi again.

Shankar, who had been watching all of this, dismounted his horse and ran towards Gauri. He took her hand as all the soldiers looked at the divine event unfold in front of their eyes. As Shankar held her hand, his body also began radiating a golden splendour. The light from the two spectral bodies merged and a bright glow spread over the battlefield, blinding everyone for a few seconds. After a moment, Shankar released Gauri's hand, having passed on all his energies to her!

Pashupati, Chandrasekhara, Gurupadaka and every other leader who witnessed the supernatural event paid obeisance to the almighty Devi Mahagauri! Anandamayi, too, sensed the same powerful energy that she had discerned when Gauri had rescued Tanmay. In that moment, she knew that the mother Goddess had indeed graced Saptapuri and its allies with her divine presence.

Invigorated by the energies of all the divinities, Gauri leapt up and landed between Anandamayi and Moishan.

'You will not stop me! I will become immortal soon! I will remain unconquered,' roared Moishan, in his strange tongue.

'You are so intoxicated with your own power and strength that you are unable to see your end, Moishan. Roar as much as you like for, I will end your evil stint on earth by slaying you here!' Gauri roared back in a tongue that every single person understood, including Moishan.

Terror flickered in Moishan's eyes as Mahagauri, the supreme embodiment of powers, came crashing down on him, her foot pressing his throat to the ground. From her backstrap, she pulled out her magnificent trishul, plunged it into his chest and simultaneously beheaded him with a sword. This was Moishan's first and last defeat!

The chants of '*Ambe Gauri*' rent the air! All men dropped their weapons and fell to their feet in complete gratitude and reverence.

A deathly silence took over as Gauri looked around her. She was standing on the headless body of a monster. Around her, the battlefield was strewn with innards, mutilated bodies and barely breathing soldiers. So much had been lost, for a greater good. She looked at Anandamayi, who was clutching the Ajna Chakra in her trembling hands.

Gauri, covered in all shades of red, looking fierce like Kaalratri (another avatar of Durga), walked towards Anandamayi and held out her left hand. Anandamayi laid on her palm a beautiful stone. It was sparking erratically and there was a buzzing charge around it. Even as the whole battlefield watched in silence, Gauri lifted the trishul in her right hand and said, 'Unchecked power is intoxicating. Uncontrolled rage, ego and greed lead to the destruction of self. Such powers do not belong in the mortal realm.'

She pierced the Ajna Chakra with the trishul. The energy released hit the trishul the way lightning strikes a metal rod, causing it to spark and vibrate. The stone crumbled and a small heap of purple grains were left in Gauri's palm. She tilted her palm, letting the stone dust mingle with the sand on the battlefield. She looked as if she had been both the storm and the one who had braved it. Shankar and Anandamayi led Gauri away from the battleground, with tears freely rolling down her cheeks.

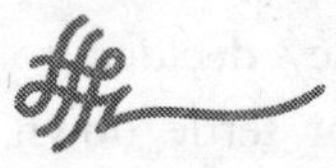

The sweet smell of victory

It was the start of a new era for the subjects of Saptapuri and all the kingdoms of the Oundin mountain range. There was much rejoicing in all the cities. News of the victory had spread far and wide. Soldiers were dispatched to the underground caves to bring the refugees home.

After the devastating war, there was much to be rebuilt. People had to recover from both the mental and physical trauma they had endured. However, the triumph of good over all that is barbaric and monstrous was something to be celebrated. Only a few knew what had actually taken place on the battlefield. Many stories were told in the days to come. The few who had witnessed the events remained silent. Nobody treated Shankar or Gauri differently. They received the usual amount of respect and veneration. Yet, the adoration and love for them had certainly grown.

Countless dead from both armies were cremated with the respect befitting martyrs. Rituals were performed and prayers were offered to send their souls to heaven. What remained of Moishan's army was a group of barbaric warriors who lacked purpose and direction in life. They had plundered, looted and killed all their lives. As far back as their memories went, they couldn't recall a time when they were not involved in war and bloodshed. With Moishan and all his generals dead, they had no leader to follow and no goals to pursue. They decided to make their way back to their lands, far away, or settle down somewhere along the way.

Manikanta had taken on the unpleasant task of purging the battlefield of the stench of flesh and rot. After several days of hard work, the fields were sanitized, but the sands remained rusty for a long time—a brutal reminder of the countless lives lost.

More than two months had passed in the blink of an eye, as the kingdom and its subjects worked around the clock to restore normalcy to their lives. Chandrasekhara, Krishnakanth, Samara, Gurupadaka, and Prajapati had all been gravely wounded by Moishan when they tried to block his attempts to reach the stone. Vidhushi performed multiple surgeries on Krishnakanth and Chandrasekhara to save their lives. She and her team worked tirelessly, often going without sleep for days, to care of the maimed and severely wounded soldiers.

Not a day went by without Vidhushi needing help from Shankar and Anandamayi. Even Maharani Gautami and Princess Indumathi were asked to pitch in. This gave Anandamayi a chance to be around Shankar, which made her very happy. Everyone assisted Vidhushi and her team in nursing the wounded back to health. All, except Gauri.

Gauri had become withdrawn and exceedingly reclusive after the war. All the death and mutilation had taken their toll on her gentle spirit. She couldn't sleep. She didn't want to eat. She didn't even want to stay inside the palace.

Every day, Gauri vividly relived every single detail of the battle. She had been an untamed and ferocious version of herself, ending a month filled with fear, hopelessness and misery by killing Moishan and his generals. But the vision of the red glazed sand, strewn with flesh and sinew from the battlefield, remained etched in her eyes. She rode to the lake each day and took long walks alone. Meditation was the only thing that helped her get through each day.

Gauri had even given up trying to find a way to get back to her world. The last time she had experimented, she came close to creating the exact chemical mix that she had decanted in the laboratory in Bengaluru many months earlier. When she had left it to rest, it began hissing and releasing the same puffs of crimson smoke that had appeared in her laboratory on that fateful day. But nothing extraordinary happened beyond that. The liquid just bubbled over and fizzled out after some time. Feeling too restless and unsettled, Gauri refused to experiment further.

Shankar had tried once to make her feel better, but he realized that her mood and spirit were too fragile to be bolstered by words. Time was the only healer for such afflictions, so he left her alone.

Pashupati organized a grand banquet in honour of all the kingdoms that had supported Saptapuri during her time of need. Invitations were sent to all the kings and their families to attend the event. Krishnakanth, Samara and Prajapati, who were still in Amara after recovering from their injuries, were joined by their families for this grand reception.

'I want everything to be perfect. It is a time for rejoicing,' exclaimed a jubilant Pashupati.

'You worry too much. Remember that the peace we have after months of strife is the true perfection,' replied Gautami. 'Every single person alive will rejoice and remember this gathering. History, too, will recall you as the king who thwarted the invaders.'

Pashupati smiled. He had done little except to keep the faith alive during this battle. Everything was a result of the inexhaustible grace of Shiva and Shakti.

The banquet was attended by all. Kings from all the kingdoms had arrived, and the commoners and subjects of the kingdom too were welcomed with open arms to be a part of the celebrations.

Pashupati stood in the great assembly hall. It was time to address his people and his guests. He had an important declaration to make.

'The sweetness of life is valued more deeply after experiencing the harsh bitterness of death and destruction. But it is not a time to dwell on the troubles we have faced. It is the hour to first honour all those who stood by us until their dying breath. These brave men have made our lives twice as precious by sacrificing their own. We will forever be indebted to their families for giving us these courageous men.'

'It is a time in our lives when we have been given a second chance to look ahead and build a bright future. There are many we must thank today: the kings and soldiers of every kingdom who took up arms to fight Saptapuri's fight; the ministers and generals for designing battle plans and tactical manoeuvres; Vidhushi and her team for providing exceptional medical care; the women and children whose patience was tested many times over; and Shankar and Gauri, the two strangers who have, over time, become our own.'

'I thank the gods for blessing me with a long and fruitful life and for the opportunity to rule and protect the people of Saptapuri. On this joyful occasion, I would like to announce that I will be stepping down from the throne and passing the kingdom of Saptapuri and its legacy to my son, Chandrasekhara.

He has demonstrated beyond doubt, especially during tough times, that he is a compassionate and capable leader. He will be crowned king on the next full moon, and I will be sending out invitations for his coronation. I once again humbly request your presence to honour him on this occasion!'

Chandrasekhara was taken aback. He had not seen this coming. His eyes moistened, glinting slightly with tears. He stood up and said, 'Thank you, Father!'

Addressing the gathering he said: 'Dear people, I promise you that I will stand with each citizen of all the allied kingdoms as we rebuild our lives together. We will restore the kingdoms of Karnikapuri and Dwajasthapura to their former glory. Kirtiswaroopam shall once again shine as the largest trading outpost in all our lands. Together, we will rise from the ashes. I will always uphold the values of humility, hard work, altruism, and our faith in one another.'

'I hope that all our esteemed guests have a hearty time today before they depart for their homes. Let us all pray that these good times last forever!'

Along with his with his gorgeous wife, Krishnakanth stood up to express his gratitude. 'Thank you Maharaja Pashupati and Crown Prince Chandrasekhara. You are truly gracious hosts, brave leaders and kind-hearted, thorough gentlemen. I came to Saptapuri's aid to bury the long-standing enmity with Maharaja Pashupati. Over the last few months, I have forged a friendship so strong that it will last for generations to come. Even in the face of instability and unrest, this kingdom, particularly the royal family, has been nothing but hospitable, kind and courageous. On behalf of every king present here, I want to thank Maharaja Pashupati and Maharani Gautami for their extreme hospitality, their willpower in leading us to victory and their attention to nursing the wounded back to health. I also want to thank my wife, Queen Tara of Karpura for stewarding our kingdom in my absence, and with efficiency.'

While speaking, he suddenly winced in pain, as he was still recovering from wounds to his abdomen. Queen Tara helped him straighten up. 'I want to thank my dear subjects, who continued to have faith in their king despite his absence and believed that their king was acting in their best interests. And finally, I express my deep appreciation and gratitude to Anandamayi, Shankar and Gauri for the immense courage and bravery they displayed on the battlefield. If it weren't for the three of them, we wouldn't be standing here thanking you all today.'

Gauri squirmed in her seat. She felt her ears becoming hot and red. She had never been the kind to call attention to herself, and all this praise being heaped on her was making her uncomfortable. Anandamayi who was seated next to Gauri reached out and held her hand, squeezing it slightly to reassure her.

'Thank you all for gracing us with your presence. It means much to us. We hope you enjoy the day, Gautami concluded the session and formally opened the grand banquet to all. The palace was soon filled with happy conversations and laughter.

Gauri silently withdrew from the celebrations and walked back to her royal chamber. The palace was far grander than the fort. Her chamber was a long walk from the banquet hall. As she was walking along a quiet corridor overlooking the garden, lost in thought, she felt a hand slip into hers. She turned to see Shankar. How he appeared so silently was beyond Gauri's understanding. He smiled at her and she returned a half-hearted smile. Shankar touched her shoulder and gently steered her away from the corridor into the gardens. He found a stone bench and sat her down.

Moonlight flooded the gardens with a soft, pearly glow. Wisps of white clouds were slowly making their way across the dark sky. The carpet of glossy black was studded with the stars. The air was perfumed with the intoxicating scent of Queen of the Night. A gentle breeze carried the fragrance to every corner of the expansive garden.

Gauri looked up at Shankar. Why did she suddenly feel a strong urge to rest her head upon his strong shoulders? To take in the scent of his skin? To close her eyes and forget the world while he put his arms around her? Why? As if he read her mind, Shankar sat down close to her and pulled her in with his left hand. He pressed her head down to his shoulder and patted it like a mother would pat her child to sleep. Gauri's heart fluttered. She had knots in the pit of her stomach, and her pulse began to race. She was scared. But it was a good scare—one filled with an anticipation, an excitement. Shankar did nothing but hold her close. He didn't say a word, letting her breathe in deeply as she rested on his bare shoulder. Gauri, whose head was nestled comfortably below Shankar's left shoulder, just above his chest, could smell the sweet, woody scent of his upper torso.

For the first time in several days, Gauri's mind stopped visualizing the battlefield. She was not thinking of the blood and gore and death and destruction. She was thinking of absolutely nothing. Not the past and not the future. She was here, in the now. With her eyes closed, she drank in the essence of her surroundings. The trees and shrubs rustled in the breeze. The crickets were intermittently making their typical throaty calls. Gauri's bare right shoulder and arm rested on Shankar's bare chest. Her right arm was tucked neatly near his hip, and her palm rested on his thighs. He brought his right hand to rest on her palm and gave it a slight squeeze. Gauri opened her eyes and looked up at his face. He bent down and kissed her forehead.

'Shankar,' she said. 'I keep reliving the past few months. I have shed more blood than all of you combined. I can't shake off the images of me beheading so many. My insides burn when I recall it all, and I wonder if life is worth living when there is so much sadness and evil around us.'

Shankar breathed in deeply. He stayed silent for a while and Gauri went back to resting her head on his chest.

'Focus on the goodness, Gauri. Amongst all of God's creations, humans are the only ones who look for a purpose in life. Look at these plants. They do not wonder about their purpose in life. They just are! They sprout, they grow and they die. Man, alone looks for a reason to live. At a basic level, our unconscious minds are entangled in our wants and needs. This gives rise to feelings of avarice, pride, inflated egos, shame, doubt and lust. In turn, these feelings can result in lies, deceit and disloyalty. A person can develop their attributes to lead a pure life, but we cannot help others to do the same. That is each person's responsibility.

'What you have done over the past few months is give each individual a chance to rise above their basic instincts and evolve to a higher level. When it became impossible for that change to occur, you helped by liberating all the negativity, giving each person a chance to be reborn and rethink their purpose in life. You are, and will always be, *Prakriti*—the primal creative force. You created it all, and you intervened when that creation was disturbed.'

'Do not let emotions like attachment and disillusionment cloud your thoughts right now. I see that the mother of all creation is doubting herself and it does not bode well for all of us. Mahamaya, the powerful goddess representing the great cosmic illusion, cannot possibly be entangled in her own *maya* (illusion), can she? Shed your darkness and look at the light you have brought into the lives of all the people around you. Tomorrow will be a different day. I promise! It seems you were supposed be here for a reason. That reason does not exist anymore.' Saying this, he kissed her forehead once again and let go of her. Gauri smiled.

Shankar stood up and began walking and Gauri followed. They went back to the banquet hall and joined the revelry. It was with a full heart and a full stomach that everyone retired that night.

Gauri felt rather light-hearted in the week that followed. She joined in for meals, spoke to people and even laughed. Nobody had seen Gauri laughing, and it was a beautiful sight. She had a child-like quality to her when she laughed with abandon at trivial things. She particularly enjoyed chatting with the young soldier Manikanta, and she treated him as one would treat their own child.

Gauri had also found a renewed calm that enabled her to her return to her experiments. She had a feeling that something would click this time around.

It was a cool, rainy afternoon when Manikanta requested an audience with Gauri. The young soldier walked into her room with a pleasant smile, and Shankar was right behind him.

'I may have found something that belongs to you, Ma!' said Manikanta. Gauri looked at him with furrowed brows. He opened his fist, and inside it was a small golden trishul. She was stunned to see the tiny charm.

She thought she had lost it after it fell into the beaker, which had exploded into crimson fumes, hurtling her into this ancient kingdom. She had never really given it much thought after she had landed here. Events had unfolded at a rapid pace after her arrival, leaving her with no time to miss a tiny little charm from her bracelet.

'Thanks Manikanta. Where did you find this?' she inquired.

'I found it on the battlefield when it was being cleaned up. It must have surfaced after the first rains. It must have dropped at the place where you magically landed during the first battle, Ma,' he added.

'I don't know what to do with it anymore, Mani. I cannot fix it back on the bracelet,' she said.

'Oh, I don't know. You may want to hold on to it, Gauri,' countered Shankar. He sounded suggestive and playful. 'By the way, how are those experiments of yours coming along?'

Gauri narrowed her eyes and punched Shankar's arm.

Manikanta excused himself and left the room.

'I had stopped, but I will try experimenting again.' Gauri said. Her excitement was palpable.

The next day, Gauri requested to meet the royal family and a few other people in the council room. When everyone had assembled, she thanked them for coming.

'It is time,' she announced. Nobody interrupted her.

'I want to thank you all for your hospitality, your belief in me and your unconditional love. It is hard for me to bid you all farewell, but I must leave. As someone told me, the time for my stay here has come to an end.' She then looked at Shankar with a twinkle in her eyes.

'I want to personally thank you all, but goodbyes have never been my forte. Prince Chandrasekhara, I wish you the absolute best as you step into your father's shoes.'

'Manikanta, stay true to yourself and someday you will make a great leader.'

'Maharaja and Maharani, your faith and love has been very comforting.'

'Vidhushi, you gave me time to grow. I thank you for your wisdom and patience.'

'Anandamayi, you are a teacher par excellence, and I am sorry I couldn't give you a gurudakshina that is worthy of you.'

'But you already have,' Anandamayi replied, looking first at Shankar and then at Gauri.

Gauri embraced her and she felt Anandamayi's tears on her shoulder.

'When the sun rises tomorrow, I will be gone. I will always fondly remember my time with you all and I hope to remain in your hearts forever.'

Tears were shed by many and Gauri remembered being embraced many times that evening. The royal family thanked her and gave her many gifts. 'Do not feel offended, but I have no use for all these treasures where I am going. I will just take small tokens to remember you all by,' she said, refusing to accept the riches and ornaments that they tried to give her.

Gauri finally left the room close to midnight. Only Shankar and Vidhushi went with her.

Vidhushi pressed a bundle into her hands. Gauri realized that it was the clothes that she was wearing when she landed on the battlefield. These were mended in some places but were fit to wear. She thanked Vidhushi and changed into them.

Shankar and Vidhushi watched as Gauri opened a wooden chest. She drew a container that was fuming crimson. She looked at the brother-sister duo, and they smiled back at her. Shankar approached her, embracing her one last time and kissed her on the forehead. 'Anandamayi will be taken care of,' he said, as he let go.

Gauri dropped the golden trishul into the fuming container and it exploded, engulfing her in crimson smoke.

My home, my realm

Thud! A loud sound scared Ananya. She was alone in the house, and the noise came from near the main door. Ananya cautiously tiptoed into the veranda but saw nothing. She walked over to the main door and looked through the peephole. She was shocked to see Gauri on the floor, just beyond the door. Ananya opened the front door in a hurry and bent down near Gauri. She called out, 'Gauri? Can you hear me? Gauri?'

When she got no response, she somehow heaved the unconscious Gauri inside and managed to place her on the sofa. She covered Gauri with a blanket and went to the kitchen. She returned with a small glass vial of reviving salts and put it near Gauri's nose.

A groggy Gauri opened her eyes, and when she saw Ananya in front of her, she felt overjoyed. She threw her hands around Ananya's neck and cried, 'Ani, it's really you! I am so glad.'

'Babe, have you lost your marbles? Of course, it is me. Is everything ok? What crazy stuff have you been smelling? And why have you been gone so long? It has been three hours, and I finished watching the first movie all alone. What happened at the lab, girl?'

'Three hours? That's it? I've been gone for only three hours?' Gauri sounded stupid.

'Look I don't know what happened at the lab, but I think you have inhaled some fumes that have affected your head. I found you on the floor outside. Just get some sleep and we can talk in the morning,' said Ananya, with a finality in her tone.

'Do you want anything to eat,' she checked with Gauri.

'No, I'm good. I'll just go sleep I guess,' Gauri replied.

As Ananya switched off the television and left for the night, Gauri pulled up her soft, snuggly blanket and closed her eyes. She drifted off into a peaceful, dreamless sleep that night.

Over the weekend, she recounted to Ananya all her escapades. Ananya refused to believe a word at first. 'I'm taking you to see a doctor. You are hallucinating wildly, and this is not a good sign,' she said. She was genuinely worried about Gauri's health.

After much explaining, Gauri managed to convince Ananya that she was not mad. She showed Ananya the keepsake trinkets that she had carried back from Saptapuri as well as her torn and mended clothes from the previous night.

It took a lot of out of Ananya to believe what Gauri was saying. Only absolute faith and trust in her friend could make her ignore all logic and believe that her friend had travelled centuries back to a different land.

Gauri for her part decided not to burden Ananya with all the details. She left out the gory killings and her ethereal transformations, making the account sound more plausible. Ananya had a lot of questions. Every day she would bombard Gauri with a spate of new questions because her story defied all logic. Gauri of course stuck to her story because what else could she do? She was recounting the truth.

At some point, a few weeks later, Ananya decided that even if she found it impossible to believe Gauri's story, she had to give her the benefit of the doubt. Gauri had become quiet and didn't speak much anymore. She wasn't her bubbly self, and Ananya felt that it was because she wasn't able to talk about her experience freely when it was always met with scepticism. So, Ananya tried her best to forget logic and just be there for her friend. She encouraged Gauri to share her experiences, but also to move forward with life now that she was back in her own territory.

'I know you want me to move on Ani. But life seems vastly different now. It seems so plain, so bleak and *sans* adventure. I don't even know where I fit in anymore. I longed to come back here all this time, back to you, amma, appa and everything familiar. Except now, I feel like I have lost something that never even belonged to me in the first place. But I wish it had, because it fit so well. I suppose this lifetime will be spent dreaming about it, wondering about it,' Gauri mused.

Ananya felt sad for Gauri. She didn't want to believe anything Gauri said, but no one could miss something so deeply if they had just imagined or concocted it. Ananya concluded that maybe it was all true. And if it was, Gauri was missing this Shankar, who she spoke of so fondly, more than anything else.

The following month at work was a busy one, and Gauri seemed to slowly ease back into her old life once again. Ananya was happy to see her getting back to the grind. It was that time of year when recruits flooded their labs due to new projects being launched. Ananya and Gauri were assigned as mentors to new employees. Gauri was excitedly chattering over lunch about how it would be great to help the new recruits, while Ananya cribbed about all the excess work.

'With all the work we already have, they are going to dump some newbies on our heads so that we can be blamed when they don't fare well. How are you so excited about this?' she asked Gauri.

'I don't know Ani, I just have a feeling,' she replied with a twinkle.

The next morning, Gauri and Ananya were having breakfast at the office canteen. Gauri had her back to the entrance, and Ananya had stepped away to bring the girls their coffee. A moment later, she heard Ananya saying, 'May I help you?'

And before Gauri could turn around, she heard the most familiar voice, a voice she had missed so much. Her heart fluttered.

'I'm looking for Gauri. I am new here, and they have assigned me to work with her. They told me to find her here. My name is...'

'Shankar?' Gauri finished the sentence. Ananya's jaws dropped. She was looking at the most handsome, ethereal-looking man!

Gauri smiled a zillion-watt smile and embraced Shankar.

'I hear that this world of yours could use some faith in god?' he whispered with a chuckle into Gauri's ears.

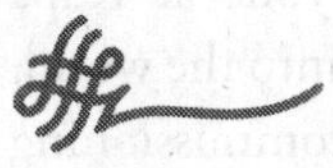

Acknowledgements

This book is, above all, an offering of gratitude. My deepest thanks go first to my late mother, Lalitha Neelakantan, whose mornings were filled with the Lalitha Sahasranamam and other devotional songs. Her voice, steady and tender, formed the earliest soundtrack of my life. Those prayers taught me rhythm, discipline, and reverence—qualities that became the quiet foundation of Mahagauri. Even though she is no longer physically present, her blessings remain the pulse behind every word I write.

To my father, S. Neelakantan, who made me a reader and showed me that books are not just paper and ink but living worlds. His unshakable faith in the power of stories has been my lifelong compass, and every chapter of this book is rooted in that early encouragement.

To my husband, Nav Pallav, and my son, Shambhav: you have been my shelter, my cheerleaders, and my silent partners in this journey. Thank you for your patience with the long nights, your understanding of my absences, and the countless small ways you created space for me to write.

My heartfelt gratitude to Suhail Mathur and The Book Bakers Literary Agency, my literary agent, who believed in this manuscript and secured this deal against all odds. To

Saswati Bora, Rudra Narayan Sharma, and everyone at Rupa Publications, thank you for shepherding this book into the world.

A special thanks to Kausalya Saptharishi, my commissioning editor, and Aparna Bhargava, copy editor, whose editorial vision and sensitivity gave Mahagauri the shape it needed.

Finally, with folded hands I thank Mahadev and Ma Durga for their continued blessings, and to my readers and well-wishers—may Mahagauri offer you the same solace and strength you have given me.